The
Feast

JENNY FARR

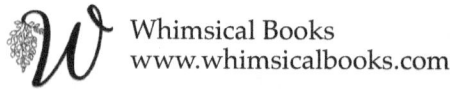 Whimsical Books
www.whimsicalbooks.com

ISBN: 978-0-578-22930-0

Book design by Jenny Farr and Justin D. Farr |
www.justinfarrdesigns.com

DEDICATION

To Justin, Joy, Valerie, and Luke

CONTENTS

ACKNOWLEDGMENTS

A million thanks to my husband for his support and encouragement, and for helping me with the book cover. Also, to my sister-in-law, Claudia, who convinced me that my story was worth sharing. Thanks to Carman for the many texts and phone calls to check on my progress and for encouraging me to finish when I felt like I couldn't. Thanks to all of my friends and my loving in-laws for their belief in me and to all of you who were so ready to read this story. Finally, thanks to my parents who instilled creativity in me and to my brother for never doubting my ability.

1. THE OPENING

O death, where is your victory? O death, where is your sting?"

A voice interrupts my singing with a boisterous, "Coco, darling!"

Standing at the solid wood table, those small but strong arms wrap around me, keeping me from unrolling the loaf of freshly baked bread from the monogrammed cloth.

"Hi, Grandma," I respond, rocking back and forth in her embrace.

I notice how smooth her olive skin is, and soft . . . almost like a baby, but still . . . mature. She gives me a kiss on my cheek and makes her way to the other side of the table to face me. Her dark brown hair falls below her shoulders in large loose curls. I'm not sure what makes her more beautiful; maybe it's her doe-like eyes that dance with expression, the only trace of age coming from wisdom that somehow beams out from her soul. Or it could be her glowing and flawless complexion, now unscarred by the years of her mortal life. She reminds me of my mother, their personalities being the only major difference between them.

Unlike mom, Grandma is an animated woman which can be surprising considering how petite she is. Everyone calls her Minnie, but her given name is Marguerite. She's the kind of woman that brings fun and laughter to everyone around her, *and* she speaks with a French accent—who doesn't like that?

She was born and raised in France, and she loves to tell us of how she fell in love with John Babin, an American from New Orleans, Louisiana. After they married she moved there and that's where they raised their two daughters—my Aunt Claire and my mother, Nicole.

My mother is quieter, like Gramps, and more reserved, and although she was raised in Louisiana, she has lost any accent that would attribute her to the area.

I, on the other hand, look completely different from most of my family living here in the Garden. I have kept my light skin, blue eyes, and blonde hair. I know, my name is Coco—it is a bit ironic. My mother is a fashion designer and named me after her inspiration whom, by the way, I have met here. Grandma told me that I look like my father's mother, both of whom I've never met, and interestingly enough, neither has she.

I unroll the bread, and the smell rises and fills our heightened senses.

"Anna sent this bread for you," I explain. "She missed you at the market today and hopes to see you tonight at the wine harvest."

"Oh, I'll be there . . . I wouldn't miss it!" she asserts loudly.

For weeks now, the wine harvest has been the focus of everyone living in the Garden. People in each community will have their own celebration where they bring in fruits and berries from the land for wine making. There will be music and dancing as usual, but this wine harvest is different. The amount of wine that will be made this harvest is more than anyone has ever made at one time. Gramps and the other builders have been building large barrels for storing it and carts for carrying the barrels. We haven't been told why yet, but we all know that something exciting is happening.

"How was the market, *ma chèrie*?" asks Grandma.

"Bustling," I reply. "It didn't take long to clear our table of teas. And everyone seemed to have extra food for sharing. The Meyers were passing out samples of their famous pistachio pudding, except this time they made it with coconut milk instead of the almond. I think I prefer the coconut."

"That sounds wonderful. And what about Ben, did he bring any of his greens?"

"He did, mustard greens cooked to perfection."

"Oh my, he can make some good greens, can't he?"

"Yes, ma'am," I reply.

Two of Grandma's favorite things about living in America were southern cooking and cajun dancing. We often have large family parties at our house, and once the accordions start playing it's hard to get her and Gramps to stop dancing. I can hear music now just thinking about it. Not accordions though—trumpets, playing in different harmonies and coming from outside. Now they stop. Grandma and I look at each other, wide smiles forming on our faces. We wait because we know what's coming next.

Bright light floods through every window in view, illuminating the lace curtains, and almost instantly the freshly cut flowers in the vase between us rise in full attention.

It's Elohim, our God.

I push the bread aside, and we run out to see the back of his chariot trailing off in the distance. "I will see you tonight at the harvest, my flowers," thunders a voice from afar.

Grandma and I wave, watching him disappear, both of us mesmerized.

"Coco!" a voice calls.

I turn to see Jense, my seventeen-year-old cousin and closest friend, running towards me. His shirt is a bright blue, the perfect contrast to his dark hair and dark eyes. At first, he runs at a human-like speed, but then—in a flash—he is before me.

I remember the first time I transported, he and I actually learned together. It was Gramps who taught us that all we had to do was think of where we wanted to go, as if we were there, and it would happen—we would actually go to that place—in an instant. It took a lot of focus at first, but we soon got the hang of it.

We can transport to any part of the Garden we'd like, but we cannot enter Alpha—Elohim's dwelling—that way; instead we must go through the gates. I could think it all that I want and it just won't happen. It's like there's an invisible shield making it impossible.

Transporting is convenient, especially when wanting to visit someone who lives miles away, but most of the time everyone moves at a human-like speed because there's so much to enjoy along the way.

Jense gives me a big hug lifting me off of my feet. We are the same age, but really he is just a big kid. I spent most of my mortal years in a boarding school, and Jense likes to tease that I'm *so mature*.

We entered the Garden at the same time and had only known each other for five months beforehand. My mother and I moved to California that year so that she could be closer to her sister. Both of their parents had already died, and the rest of their extended family were living in France. Mother took me out of the boarding school to live with her in California. Something had changed in her, which now I know was the Lord's doing. For years she was so focused on her work and traveling that she lost contact with her sister, and with me, really. But she said she wanted to change that, and she did. No one knew our time together would be so short.

Jense's mother, Aunt Claire, had given me a ride to the church's youth group that night, and on our way home an out of control truck rammed into the side that Jense and I were on. I was sitting in the back to the right side where the truck made most impact, and I passed immediately. I saw Yeshua, or as we knew him on earth—Jesus, running to me. Jense didn't die immediately. He was strapped into the passenger side with only enough time to see that his mother was alive and to say a quick prayer asking the Lord to save him. Knowing that his mother watched him die was more than his spirit could bear. He had so much turmoil going on inside when we arrived to see Elohim. But with one touch he was made whole. There's something about Elohim's touch that makes your questions feel like they're answered. Just one touch and your soul is settled for good. Jense was settled, and later Elohim let him go to his mom in a dream, telling her that he was alive and well.

After our introduction to our new heavenly home, Jense and I met our grandparents whom we dwell with today. We were young when they died, too young to remember them, but it didn't take long for us all to get acquainted. Now, it feels like we've known them forever.

We live on a tea plantation in the community called

Epsilon. Our family's land is comparable to the size of a small city, and houses generations of family members. Our house sits inland from the coast about fifteen miles.

There are seven communities that make up the Garden. Alpha is in the center and all of the other communities—Beta, Gamma, Delta, Epsilon, Digamma, and Zeta—encircle Alpha expanding out until they each reach a coast. It is in Alpha that the highest of all mountains dwells; it is the Holy Mountain where Elohim's palace sits on the very top. His light is what gives us our days, and at night, large clouds create a staggering descent so that his light becomes dim and it even gets dark, unlike how I'd ever imagined it would be like. The clouds make it dark for us, but above the clouds, Elohim's palace always stays lit with his radiating light. We do have a sun for warmth and even a distant moon and stars. Night time in the Garden is never scary though—it's magical. It is never completely dark but enough to appreciate light shows from the lightening bugs and firework displays. Hanging lanterns light the paths throughout the land and turn on at night, and the stars take turns with the crickets making quiet music to our God.

Families generally stay in the same communities, and like ours, they share the same land; however, some dwell in different parts of the Garden depending upon their enjoyments and other relationship factors. Because we can arrive anywhere in a flash, it makes visiting really easy, and that takes the pain out of being apart. Some of our family have chosen to live closer to their spouse's family. We, immortals, no longer marry, but those married as mortals stay together as a family because relationships built on earth are just as important here. It's different though, and hard to explain to a mortal who has not been made completely whole. There is no physical or sexual attraction but only a brotherly or sisterly sort of love for one another. I have never married and I never will, and as hard as it may be to believe, there is nothing sad or lacking about that. I am completely satisfied and completely whole.

The house that Jense and I share with our grandparents looks like a small plantation house. It is two-story and white, with dark green shutters, and columns along the bricked front porch. Honeysuckle vines climb up the end columns; you can smell their sweet fragrance from the nearby double swing, on which I share many nights with Grandma. The first level is completely open with wooden floors and throw rugs that Grandma and I made ourselves. An overstuffed couch, a chaise, and a matching pair of floral armchairs fill in the living area, and there's even a kitchen with all of the conveniences one would want for cooking.

Food does not spoil in the Garden, but it is constantly regenerating itself. And our necessity for food is different here. Unlike our mortal bodies that needed calorie intake per day to sustain itself, here we eat to sustain our spirits— especially when we go to Alpha to visit the Holy Mountain. The fruit from the trees keep us strong in Elohim's presence, but along with that, eating and drinking is for pleasure and for sharing with one another.

Elohim loves variety, so he has made the Garden a home of many types of plant life for us. Our plantation sits at the base of lush mountains with streams flowing through the land and large, deep swimming holes with water falls and caves surrounding them. There is an abundance of tall trees —many are fruit trees, acting as a canopy over the smaller fruit and nut trees. The peppervines and other types of vines climb their way up the trees creating what looks like a waterfall of leaves. Shrubs of currants and berries fill in the spaces around them. Herbs and vegetables make their homes together along with the ground covers which spread their way throughout the land. It is very green in Epsilon.

Jense grabs my hand. "The water is up! Let's go!"

Grandma nods and gently pushes us. "You kids go

ahead. I'll get Gramps and we'll see you at the Opening."

The *Opening*—it's spectacular really. There is a river separating each community that branches off into streams making its way through the Garden and watering the land. When the river rises, the vines which grow along their sides climb up the nearby trees and wrap their way around the hanging wind chimes, causing a domino effect of chiming throughout the land. It's our Lord's way of letting us know there is an Opening. You'll see what I mean.

Jense and I run through the grass laughing, and together we jump across the stream. Suddenly, the forms of our bodies change so that it appears we are wearing running clothes. Here, our eyes, hair, and skin coloring stay true to our mortal bodies. But with a thought, our bodies can take on different forms of clothing. Also, the shade of color we choose to wear will change depending upon our level of excitement. I am radiating shades of yellow, and Jense, shades of blue. Right now, because we are running, my yellow shirt is bold and bright like a canary. Jense and I both appear to wear black running shorts, and we are barefoot as always. We do not wear handmade clothing here, only Yeshua. He is the only one with a resurrected body. The rest of us must wait for our human bodies to be resurrected when he returns to Earth again. Until then, we are spirit, only reflecting the image of a body, and everything in our realm is an image—the food, the clothing, all objects around us, and yet we can experience them with all of our senses.

I love the feeling of the grass between my toes and the way the air kisses my skin as I run. Along the way, we grab handfuls of berries—blackberries, raspberries, and mulberries. Their sweetness fills our mouths and spreads throughout our bodies.

We take a narrow path of bluebell wood. It's a flooring made of blue flowers, and in this case, it's between walls of tall trees. At the end of the path we enter an open yard of grass, encircled with bushes of golden showers and jungle flames. Their yellow and bright-red colored flowers only intensify our excitement. Suddenly, they begin to make music. The golden showers play flute notes like an algoza, and the jungle flames make tapping drum beats. Together they create an upbeat melody and their fragrance becomes visible. What appears to be colored smoke, rises above them in dancing motions and continues towards the Holy Mountain where they will make their way to the throne room of Elohim's palace. I jump with excitement, and we take off running again. This time down a grassy path through the woods until we come to our favorite swimming hole, hidden amongst caves with a long-dropping waterfall. Gramps and Grandma appear from a different path. We wave and smile at one another. Gramps, wearing a white t-shirt, and Grandma in a glowing magenta, have the bodies of mortals in their prime, except without limits. Gramps looks strong and boyish as he takes off running with Grandma following, and they jump to the other side of the water. Jense can wait no longer. He jumps high above the water, flips twice, and dives down deep into the hole. I dive in behind him and our eyes meet. We can read each other's thoughts under water, and we can stay under as long as we'd like. Smiling, we swim next to each other until we surface behind the waterfall.

I grab onto the large, wet rocks and pull myself up. Sitting next to Jense and looking into the waterfall . . . we see the Opening.

When Elohim allows, we can look into any body of water and he will give us a glimpse into the mortal world. We may not see the same thing as the person next to us. Instead, he gives us a look into the lives of our own families or at things that would be important for us to see. It keeps us connected to what he is doing on the earth. This is a time when a full range of emotions are felt, and we are allowed to speak to their souls. We do not speak so that they hear, but our spirit cries to theirs; we cheer them on and speak encouragement to them. Time is altogether different here compared to there, so during the Opening, the Lord takes us to that moment in their time.

As I gaze into the waterfall, I see my father. His name is Marten Alvin Lindstrom; Yeshua told me. I like the sound of Coco Lindstrom—it seems so sophisticated—but I have always been proud to carry my grandpa's last name. I have never met him, and this is only my second time to see him through the Opening. I look like him.

He sits at his drawing table holding a magnifying glass. My father is an artist, and it looks like he is inspecting his newest work. As he backs away, I can see the painting. My shirt begins to radiate a yellow that is higher on the scale of coloring. It is a painting of Yeshua, and pretty accurate too. I am beaming from joy as the Lord speaks and says to me, "He is a believer, my dear. You will meet him one day." My excitement is so high that I shoot up through the waterfall, blow kisses to my God—who I know can see me—and return to my spot on the rocky ledge.

"Well done, dad," I speak out to him. "You have made the right choice. Be strong in your faith because the Lord has heard you."

My glimpse into mortality fades, and the sounds of muttering takes my attention to Jense.

I grab his hand so that I can see into his thoughts. Aunt Claire is crying, alone in her bed. I instantly understand that Jenses' parents are getting a divorce and his father has already left her. We hear Elohim's voice speaking kindly to him, "I hold your mother's tears in a bottle. I know her pain." Jense remains silent, and the tears that have fallen from her eyes join together and take on the form of a glass bottle. It lifts away from her and disappears.

Jense, now filled with hope, says, "Mom, you are so

loved, and the Lord will work everything out for the good. Be encouraged." For a moment his mother is still, and we know that her spirit received it. Jense's muted blue coloring becomes a brighter shade. We smile and I hug him tightly.

Gramps and Grandma make their way through the waterfall and take a seat next to us, and it's just like Grandma to have encouraging words ready at the right time.

"There is a day coming when this will be over—the pain." She recites from memory verses out of the Holy Book saying, "*He will wipe away every tear from their eyes, and death shall be no more, neither shall there be mourning, nor crying, nor pain anymore, for the former things have passed away. . . . Heaven and earth will pass away,*" Jense joins her in concluding, "*but my words will never pass away.*"

We sit and ponder the verses. These are living words— true words. Everything will pass away—even the Garden where we live today. See, even now we can feel pain because the fallen world still exists. The only difference is we have the understanding through it. But the Holy Book tells us of a day when there will be no more pain. A day when heaven and earth as we know it will be made new.

"We have much to look forward to," Jense replies.

"Yes, son, we do," Gramps agrees.

2. THE PROCLAMATION

There is a buzz in our community. Multitudes of excited people are entering the wide, open field from the paths of the woods. Some are carrying large baskets of grapes and berries to add to those already gathered.

Jense and I are sitting in the grass taking in the moment. My mint green sun dress falls around me, and Jense has the form of white linen pants and sort of an oyster colored polo shirt. He sits with his legs crossed, pulling up grass with his hands. We are facing a large, empty platform. Above the trees to the left and right of us, and straight ahead above the platform are stories and stories of balconies. In each box section of the balconies are bands of musicians and singers.

At the moment there is no singing, only the musicians playing in harmony with one another, each, at the right moment, giving their own flavor and style. The way it all blends together seems impossible.

Jense taps me on the leg and points in the lower balcony where he spotted our friends, Sam and Abby. They both have the skin color of dark chocolate and smiles of ivory. Their family owns the land that neighbors ours, and their father is Ben from the market. Their entire immediate family is here in the Garden since their time dated back hundreds of years before ours. Their mother, Sarah, and both of their grandmothers, Sena and Eugenie, sew with my grandmother. Sena leads a sewing group for our community, and whenever someone new enters they bring monogrammed linens to them as a welcoming gift.

Abby is holding her saxophone waiting patiently, and, as if on cue, Sam begins playing the bass guitar.

I have never been one to play an instrument. In fact, not many in my heritage do. Instead, we express ourselves through painting, sewing, and, in Gramp's case, building. Jense is all together different. He's an athlete. He heads up activities for many of the children in our community. Some days they play a sport, but mostly he takes them surfing. Jense was a champion surfer as a mortal, which made him very popular in school. I'm sure his good looks had something to do with that too. Our family loves going to the coast where I lie in the sand while Jense surfs the waves. Sometimes we dive down deep to gather shells. It is not dark underwater here, even in the deep. Instead it's bright with colorful fish and boldly colored coral, especially at night.

The music begins to lower in sound, and one by one each musician fades out. This gives everyone the chance to stop talking and take their seat in the grass of the open field. Our attention is now straight ahead as bright flashes of light begin appearing behind the platform until the empty space is completely filled with angels. If it weren't for their glow and the fact that they all wear white, you may mistake them for a really tall human.

They are very interesting creatures who can radiate light, brighter than a mortal human can stand to look at. And just as we are able to change our form as wearing clothing, angels are able to change their form on earth as appearing to be human. They are not always as bright as they are today. They actually have the ability to dim their light on occasion. But because they are appearing so bright now, we know they are preparing us to see Elohim.

The number of angels in the Garden are beyond my knowledge. There are just too many to count. The archangels, on the other hand, are less in number but higher in hierarchy. They are very much honored and respected among the angels, like any commanding officer would be. They stand about ten feet tall and they have two large wings. The archangel Gabriel now appears on stage with a trumpet in his hand. He is very much as I'd imagined as a kid when I'd heard the story of Christ's birth—blonde hair, tall and strong, and illuminating bright light. He has a set of two large white wings and wears a white robe. Gabriel blows the trumpet and everyone is quiet.

The recognizable sound of rushing wind, like the flapping of large wings, comes from the east, and then we see it. A large, red chariot appears with Elohim on his golden throne and Yeshua seated at his side on a similar throne. The chariot is big enough to hold the both of them, but it is not pulled by horses or anything visible to our eyes. It is carried by creatures that we cannot see. I am told that they can only be seen at the palace if they so wish to show themselves. The chariot stops on the platform and everyone begins to cheer.

They are both wearing white robes as well, but they

couldn't look any more different from one another. When Elohim is around us, he takes on the form of a superior man with white hair and a white beard. He is somehow stately and unrefined all at once, as if the Greek gods were fashioned after him. And though he takes the form of a man, there is not the appearance of flesh and bones like the rest of us humans; it is more like glass carrying bright light. He's sort of like a light bulb when it's turned on. When you look at it there is the form of the glass—a shape—but the light fills the form and goes out of it. That is what Elohim is like yet in the shape of a man. But unlike a light bulb that would be too hot to touch, you can touch Elohim. This is the way that he presents himself to us, in a form that we can relate to —as a man, so that we can have relationship with him.

Unlike Elohim, Yeshua *was* a man and therefore has real flesh and bones, with light-brown skin and sort of burly brown hair and matching beard. His green eyes dance with joy at the sight of all of us here. Yeshua is our king and is treated as such by all. He stands to his feet, and in unison the angels fall down, their faces parallel with their knees. Laugh lines appear on his face as he smiles and stretches out his hands to greet us.

"Welcome to our Annual Wine Harvest Celebration!" he calls out. All of the horns and drums burst forth from the balconies; we applaud and cheer loudly.

Epsilon's wine harvest has always been a big deal, but this one feels different, and by the looks of things we can tell there is an important announcement to be made. Especially now that Michael, the archangel, appears on stage. At the sight of him, the cheering quickly diminishes, and everyone begins whispering and peering to get a good look at the famed archangel.

He has dark hair, and his body is like chiseled iron. A long, red cape is cloaked around him as he stands quietly next to Yeshua with his head bowed. It is a rare event for

Michael to be called—away from his warriors—to the Garden.

I look at Jense with wonder; he sits up straight—wide-eyed and attentive. A hush falls upon the crowd as Yeshua takes his seat, and Elohim begins to speak.

"Thank you, children, for your involvement in the wine harvest, as always. Look at all of this! Fantastic," he says, motioning to the many rows of baskets and barrels of berries. "As you may know, we have asked for larger amounts of wine to be made this time. Yeshua and the builders have made carts and barrels for storing, and many of you have carried in the finest of grapes and berries." He pauses and his eyes become tender. "Thank you. This is a time for celebrating, but unlike the previous years, things are getting ready to change. It is a good change. Something we have all looked forward to for ages. I'd like Gabriel to explain." He directs his right hand toward Gabriel, and this time with a powerful voice that takes us all by surprise he commands, "Gabriel, begin the proclamation."

The bowed angels stand as Gabriel steps forward from his place at Elohim's left side and blows his trumpet. Bumps form on my arms as a chill runs through my body.

With a loud and resounding voice he proclaims, "As per request of the Almighty, preparation for the Great Feast begins!"

There is a gasp and then a hush. Everyone in the Garden knows what Gabriel is referring to. The Great Feast has been spoken of for generations but always as a future event. Now, here in this moment, the preparation for this event has begun. The Holy Book tells us of a time when Yeshua will return to Earth to gather his people and mark a change of life on Earth as we have all known it. After reuniting with our families, we will celebrate with a feast.

Gabriel continues, "Though you do not know the time of its occurrence, preparations are to begin from this day forward with each person giving according to their own gifting. The Holy Book foretold that it shall be *a feast of rich food for all peoples, a banquet of aged wine — the best of meats and the finest of wines.* Up until this time there has been no hunting or eating of meat in the Garden, but now the Lord has prepared the land of Alpha at the base of the Holy Mountain, stocked with only the best animals created for such a time as this. Along with the grass fed bovines which are kept on the hills, there are new beasts, unknown to man, and kept within the forest—the new cervidae and wild ovine; also the pip and the pose, pheasants of the finest. There is a barrier keeping the animals separated from all other animals of the Garden. Only these animals are to be hunted and used for the Great Feast, and the barrier will have no affect on you or your transporting."

He looks in our direction, peaking my attention even more.

"Sena," he says, looking almost through me at Sam and Abby's great-grandmother. "The Lord is calling upon all tailors, seamsters, and seamstresses to create white linen robes. Please come forward.

Sena, a large, but fit, woman walks forward smiling, and in a flash she stands before Gabriel. He places his right hand on her head. "The patterns are given to you now. Share them with the others."

She walks back to her seat, this time much slower, and it is clear that she is looking at the image or images that have been downloaded in her mind. We are all curious to see what she sees. She takes her seat on a blanket and clasps hands with Eugenie. Eugenie sighs with delight as the vision in Sena's mind passes to hers. I am glad that my grandmother will soon see the robes and hopefully share them with me. I search the crowds and find her sitting next to Anna, and we smile at each other with excitement.

The proclamation continues.

"Every person that would like to prepare food should begin bringing to market for all to taste. Only the best should be prepared for the Great Feast. This will require input and involvement from everyone in the community. Once meals have been decided upon, begin making and storing large portions.

Winemakers, you are to begin your process following tonight's festivities. Gather the aged wine of previous harvests and store them with the new wine, each specifically labeled as aged or new.

All others will be given personal instructions in a nearer time. Everyone, rejoice and be merry!" And now with an almost booming effect that reaches the core of my being he proclaims, "Let the preparations begin!"

Everyone cheers as he blows his trumpet and takes a step back next to Elohim. Yeshua stands, and the musicians begin to play a jazz number that reminds me of Mardi Gras in New Orleans. People jump to their feet and begin dancing, and Yeshua comes down from the platform to join in. Elohim belts out a hardy laugh as he watches his children rejoicing. I am not sure how long this lasts. Song after song we dance and make great noise. My dress twirls as I spin, and in the corner of my eyes I see people jumping wildly around me. Dancing next to me is a young girl named Ling. She grabs my shoulder, as I realize everyone is doing, so I grab onto Jense. Clasped together, our whole community jumps up and down. We laugh like children as many of us get off beat and fall over causing others to fall with us. Piling on top of each other, we remain on the ground in hysteria, and then slowly the music comes to an end. We are all laughing like inebriated fools.

The trumpet sounds for the last time. We stand somewhat staggering and see Elohim and Yeshua now seated on their thrones with Gabriel and Michael fixed behind them. They wave and begin to leave, so we wave back and cheer again. Many blow kisses and shout out praises as the chariot takes off. One by one the angels disappear taking what's left of the bright light with them. As the last of the angels leave, the lanterns in unison turn on around the field and throughout our community. The stars are twinkling, and the singers in the bandstands begin to quietly sing songs of worship. People pack their belongings to leave, and the winemakers gather the baskets to begin their process.

Jense and I bend down to gather our few items from the soft grass, still bubbling from the celebrating. I hear my name being called and look up to see our friend, Leslie, running towards us.

"Hey, wanna go to the beach?" she asks. Her white button up shirt blows lightly in the breeze, brushing against her khaki shorts. I'm not surprised to see her wearing a woven sun hat because making hats is something Leslie loves to do. This hat has beautiful braided details with a large red hibiscus and is sitting on top of her thick, medium-length blonde curls. Leslie is also seventeen and lives with her family on the coast. She grew up in middle America and came to the Garden in 1962, so it's super fun to hear her talk with the slang that she uses. She likes to say words like *golly* and *jeepers*, the types of things I had only heard on old TV shows.

"I'd like to go," I reply. "Jense?"

He nods. "Yeah, that'd be great."

In a flash, we are standing at the water's edge. My toes sink into the cool, wet sand, and the water reaches in and sweeps over our feet. It's just the right temperature as always. Bold colors of hot pinks, purples, and blues pop from below the deeper parts of the waters. It's so clear that I can see the fish and the vibrant plant life swaying with the current. I zoom my sight in on a group of florescent yellow fish. I can even see the small, barely visible, white dots on their backs.

Leslie is giggly and talkative as usual, but I notice that Jense is suddenly being very quiet. Maybe it's because he hasn't had a chance to get a word in between the two of us girls, but I'm almost positive that something is on his mind.

"So, Les, what are you going to do for the Great Feast?" I ask, trying to bring the conversation to a place where Jense can join in too.

"Well," she says in a girlish sort of voice. "I would love to help with making the table settings. I'm thinking tall, elaborate flower arrangements with flowers that cascade down onto the table and then smaller, simpler arrangements around it. What about you?"

"Does taste testing count?" I ask. We both laugh and look at Jense who lets out a short, blow through the nose type of laugh, and now I know he is contemplating something.

"What are you thinking about?" I ask him.

Jense smiles, eyes remaining serious, and takes a few seconds before he speaks. "You know that after the feast there is the Great War?" He is not worried or fearful as a mortal man might be, instead he is standing tall with a fierceness in his eyes. "I am ready to fight with Yeshua and bring an end to evil for good."

Les and I are quiet. Jense is right—after our feast there will be a war led by Yeshua on Earth. We already know that we will win; it has been foretold. There's no fear or worry, but there's so much anticipation because before the war, Yeshua will return to Earth to gather his people—our families—to bring them here to the Garden, and we will all finally be together.

"That means that the Gathering is coming . . . like really soon!" I can't hide my excitement as I speak, and my body proves it even more. Now Les and Jense are both beaming along with me. Our excitement is tangible. I can remember in my mortal body there were times that I was so excited my spirit wanted to jump out of my body. Now I am spirit. No mortal body refraining me. I could jump so high at this moment to think that the time is finally coming. To hold my mother again and meet my father. Knowing that Satan, our enemy, could never deceive or hurt again. Knowing that we can all be one whole family living in a world that is ruled by Yeshua himself.

Our clothing turns bright hues and we are glowing— green from me, white from Leslie, and a bright orange from Jense. The three of us shoot up into the sky in flips of all sorts. I imagine that we look like a firework show above the water.

"Whoo!" shouts Jense. "Yeah!"

We fall down gracefully and land on our feet.

"Wow, I can't believe it," says Leslie. "Tell me this really is true." She fixes her curls beneath her hat as we collapse next to each other, close enough so that our arms are touching.

Jense and I know Leslie's story, how she married Jimmy at sixteen and died a year later after giving birth to their baby girl, Evelyn. She happily watched Jimmy remarry Liz years after her death, and she's seen Evelyn grow into a beautiful woman with her own family, all through the Opening. It's hard to explain how Leslie could be happy about Jimmy's marriage, or how she could be okay with missing all of those years with Evelyn. One would have to understand the satisfaction and fulfillment that is here in the Garden I guess, or the perfect love of Elohim that is not selfish or self-seeking. Les once told me that she waits for the day to hug Jimmy's neck and to thank him for taking care of Evelyn and giving her a mom like Liz.

We sit for a time without talking, each of us lost in our own thoughts.

"It's true," I finally say, lightly bumping my shoulder against hers. She smiles and bumps back a little harder so that I knock into Jense. Just as any big brother would, Jense tackles the two of us and begins tickling us so that our feet are flinging sand everywhere.

"Stop!" We yell, laughing and fighting against his grip. He lets go and jumps to his feet still smiling mischievously. "I'm going home now, you coming, Co?"

I sigh and brush the sand off of me. "Yes, we should." I help Leslie up and she gives me a tight squeeze.

"I hope you get to help with arranging the tables," I say. "I know you will do a beautiful job."

"Thanks, Coco . . . and maybe I will see you at the market tomorrow. I have plenty of hats."

3. PREPARATION

The smell of cardamom hits me as I enter the clearing. My bare feet step onto the cool, cobblestone pavement, and I hear the chatter and laughter of the busy market. Everyone is excited about the upcoming feast. Rows and rows of booths, some covered and some uncovered, offer the best goods of the land. There is no buying or selling here. Everyone in the Garden has something to offer and we give freely to each other. Usually we make a trade as a courtesy, but it isn't necessary. There is no fear of running out of anything because the Garden is made to flourish and give abundantly. The land is so rich that the crops produce on their own, so there is no hard work or toiling. We only gather and share.

I have my baskets full of tea leaves. Gramps made side-baskets to fit on the back of my miniature horse, Dolly. She was a present from Elohim, waiting for me at the plantation when I first arrived in the Garden. I always wanted a miniature horse, but it was impossible to have one at the boarding school. It was one of those unanswered prayers, or so I thought at the time. Then I realized he answered me in the best way possible because now, Dolly will never die. I will not lose her. She is mine.

I was delightfully surprised by the animals here. Not only was Dolly waiting, but also the prettiest, long-haired cat you ever did see was curled up on my bed. I named him Lansing for no apparent reason, it's just what came to me when I saw him. I asked Grandma how this was so—animals and pets—and she said that they were resurrected from the earth. Not every animal resurrects, but only those that Elohim choses. Leslie's childhood dog, Peanut—he's here too.

I pull Dolly along down the row ahead of me. The sound of her feet clocking on the cobblestones makes almost a musical beat to accompany the flute players at a nearby booth. They have ropes of garlic and peppers hanging from their canopy and little wooden flutes laid out on a table. Next to them, Silvia and Raymond display their assortment of wind chimes. I pass my hand across them as I walk by and the sound of deep, woody tones mix in with the chiming of the smaller ones. Another smell hits me—freshly baked, warm bread.

"Hi, Anna," I say as I stop at the wooden table. I pull the monogrammed linen cloth from a pouch on Dolly's back.

"Hi, Coco, and hello there, Dolly," she returns. Dolly shakes her head of long hair, and her tail brushes against her back leg.

"She is happy to see you." I say, and hand her the cloth.

"Thanks again for the bread."

"Oh, you are welcome." She runs her hand across the monogram. It is a capital A for Anna. "I am so excited that Minnie gets to help make the robes. Did she show you what they are going to look like?" she asks.

I smile and nod. "Here, take my hand."

As I hold her hand, the images that I saw when I held my grandmother's hand are now in Anna's mind—long and airy, white linen robes that swoop down in the back just below the shoulder blades and continue to the floor, ending in a small, flowy train.

She smiles wide and sighs. "They are beautiful," she says in a dreamy sort of way. "But what about the men?"

"You know, I'm not sure." I didn't think much about it. Probably because the beauty of the robes that I saw draped upon the multitudes of women and young girls was striking enough on its own.

"Huh. Well, thank you for showing me . . . and please, taste my tapas and tell me what you think."

"Ummmm," I say after taking a bite. "It's crispy with a nice buttery taste, and the tomatoes and basil give the perfect amount of sweetness. I like."

"Oh good," she says.

"Here, I have something for you." I pull out a small pouch from one of my baskets. "A mixture of green tea and spearmint leaves."

"Well, I will enjoy this. Thank you, sweetie. Tell Minnie 'hello' for me, would ya?"

"Yes, ma'am, I will."

I take Dolly's lead rope and continue past the many booths and tents. I can see my spot ahead, but first there's a large wagon holding different types of vegetables and fruits. I offer a pouch of tea bags as a trade for an apple. As I take a bite, the juice spills onto my tongue and pleases my sense with its sweet liquid. I always liked apples before, but eating apples on earth are no comparison to what its like here. Everything is that way. Even the cajun food that my mother grew up on in New Orleans cannot compare to how good food tastes here.

"Salut, Coco! J'ai fait de la place sur la table . . . . ." she speaks to me in French, but I understand every word of it. My great-grandmother tells me that she made room on the table for my dried tea leaves. Her name is Brigitte, but Jense and I call her Gigi. She and her sister, Noemi, brought potted herbs to market today. Both women are slender, but Noemi is about six inches taller. They have the same complexion as my grandma and my mom, with brown hair and brown eyes, and they live together in a small house near ours. Neither of their husbands entered the Garden, but each of their children and most of their families are here and live close to us. On our land we grow teas of different varieties, but we also grow herbs to accompany the teas. Today, Gigi and Aunt Noemi brought a selection of sweet fennel, lemon balm, spearmint, and rosemary.

On tending days, Jense helps our cousins with drying the tea leaves and assorting them, and I make the organza drawstring pouches that we separate them into. I like to get the gold colored organza from Hari who trades me for a tea that is similar to Darjeeling. Hari loves Darjeeling.

Gramps made me a stamp for my pouches with the image of a teapot with intricate details that almost look like lace. My younger cousins, Letty and Lion, help me with the stamping. Letty was miscarried and is now reunited with her mother, my cousin Christy, and Lion lives with them. He was aborted and his mother is still a mortal. She never named him, so we call him Lion after Yeshua. The Holy Book uses animals to describe Yeshua's character, the lion being one of them.

It seemed to be a fitting name for the little boy who loves to pretend being ferocious. All babies brought into the

Garden are advanced to the size and understanding comparable to a five year old, so it was easy to see the personality that Lion already possessed. And though children in the Garden advance in their learning and knowledge as we all do, their innocent love for play and fun remains. Letty and Lion bring so much joy and fun to our family. I can't imagine not having them here.

"Yeshua!" someone shouts. I turn to see him approaching down the street on his horse named Oleksander, a large white stallion. How unexpected it is to see him here today.

Horns and flutes from the nearby market musicians give welcome to our king, and we clap our hands, so happy that he is here. Oleksander comes to a stop and stands still in full attention as Yeshua dismounts with ease. His white shirt stands out against the tan riding pants; tall black boots reach up below his knees. The feeling I have when I see him is like a child excited to see their big brother coming home from a long trip. I just saw him last night, but still I feel that way now.

He is very polite saying "hello" to everyone, but he keeps walking towards me smiling.

"Coco!" he calls, extending his arms towards me. "You are just who I was looking for."

"Really?" I am pleasantly surprised and run into his brotherly embrace.

"Of course," he says, and pats me on the head. "I'd like to have a meal at your house tonight. I have something important to discuss with you."

"We would be honored," I reply with a huge smile.

"Great. I will see you tonight when the black birds sing."

"Okay, I'll see you then."

He waves at Gigi and Aunt Noemi, then turns to leave.

I stand holding my arms, watching him mount Oleksander. Then after waving again to everyone, he turns the stallion and is gone in an instant. I run to my great-grandmother.

"You must get home and prepare, dear," she tells me. "Noemi and I will be here. Leave everything—we will bring Dolly back for you."

"Thank you, Gigi." I pull a canvas bag from one of my baskets and quickly make a few trades for fish, sweet potatoes, and salad fixings.

I transport to the doorway of the community center where Grandma is sewing with the others.

"Grandma!" I say, running through the open doorway.

"Yes, *bébé*?" She looks up with a needle between her teeth.

"Yeshua is coming for supper. He wants to talk to me about something important."

Grandma immediately gathers her things, and together we transport to the plantation to make preparations.

✦

Gramps, Grandma, Jense, and I sit at the wooden table which is dressed with our best place settings, awaiting Yeshua's arrival. The windows are open, and a breeze blows the lace curtains away from their place against the wall. Jense is tapping his fingers, Gramps starts to whistle, and then the black birds sing. There is a knock on the door.

I race Jense to answer it, and with both of us reaching, we grab the knob at the same time. We are laughing as we open the door and welcome Yeshua in.

"Hi, Coco. Hi, Jense. John and Minnie, thank you for having me in your home."

"Of course, Lord, it is our pleasure," says Gramps. They embrace in a short but heartfelt hug. Then Yeshua and Grandma kiss each other's cheek.

"Please, have a seat at the table," offers Grandma; Jense pulls the chair out for him. I pour everyone a glass of cold, sweet tea as Grandma serves portions onto the plates. I would serve the finest wine for our Lord, but everyone knows that he made a promise to not drink any until the day of the Great Feast.

Grandma's salmon is my favorite, but my mind is too preoccupied to notice its flavor. I eat mechanically as Gramps and Yeshua talk building plans between bites. Jense listens intently and occasionally joins in, while Grandma and I wait patiently for what the Lord really came to say. Of course, he knows this and glances at the two of us and smiles. He wipes his mouth, and he and Gramps finish their conversation. Jense suddenly has much to say, so Grandma and I continue to endure as the Lord answers his questions, mostly pertaining to hunting. It's the big topic right now because there has never been a hunt here in the Garden. He wants to know about the new animals—how many we are allowed to kill, what is the best way to kill them, on and on. It is actually very interesting, and I decide that I want to go with Jense on a hunt.

Grandma interrupts by placing the Madeleines on the table.

"Would you like coffee or tea, Lord?"

"I want your favorite tea, Minnie."

"My favorite? Well, that would be the Du Hammam."

"Perfect," he says.

"I will help," I offer, standing until his hand covers mine.

"Actually, Coco, you and I have matters to discuss."

He retrieves his hand, but the warmth remains. I gladly sit back down.

"Yes, Lord?"

"Coco, have you seen the linen robes that your grandmother and the others are making?"

"Yes, I have seen them. They are lovely."

"And have you seen the pattern for my robe?"

"No, I don't believe I have."

"That's because I don't have one. That is what I want to

discuss with you."

"Me, Lord?"

"Yes, I want you to design my robe, and I want you to make it for me."

"I only know how to sew pouches."

"I know," he says, smiling.

"I've never made a garment before."

"Exactly," he responds, confident and beaming.

"This has to be the greatest honor. Why me, Lord?"

"Why not?" he responds. Then in a little bit louder voice he asks, "So, Coco, will you make my robe for me?"

"Yes!" I say, because I know that he sees something I do not see. I know that he wouldn't ask unless he knew that I could do it, and because I want this to be an act of worship to him. "I am honored."

"And so am I."

Grandma comes carrying a tray with her favorite green tea, sprinkled with flower petals. The fragrant smell of roses mixed with berries and oranges suddenly fills the room.

I'm realizing that I need to discuss logistics with him while I can. "So, Lord, will you wear this robe to battle as well as to the feast?"

"Yes, I will celebrate in it, and I will most definitely battle in it . . . if that is what you want to call it," he says playfully.

"Well, it is called the Great War—*isn't it*?"

"Yes, you are correct. That is what it has been coined. I personally like to think of it as more of a seize control."

"Of course," I humbly respond. I understand that along with being playful, he is also teaching me something important. Yeshua holds all power over all of his enemies, so he is reminding me that the upcoming war is really nothing more than him showing up and taking over. I wonder if there will even be a battle, or if by his very presence they will fall in defeat. I try to picture it—men, mere mortals, coming to fight God Almighty. How could they ever think that they could win? Of course, the crafty one, the deceiver —Satan himself—will be the instigator of their rebellion.

"You will know what to make, Coco, just follow your intuition."

His words are believable so I simply say, "Okay," as Grandma respectfully interrupts. "Would you be more comfortable in the living area?"

"That sounds nice, thank you."

We lounge in coinciding chairs, and the others join us now. Seeing that our discussion is over, Grandma is back to her loud mannerisms. She tells us stories from her sewing group, and then Jense and I talk about the children and surfing. Our conversation jumps from there to the wine harvest. Yeshua wants to know our reaction as we heard Gabriel's proclamation and what we thought of Michael, the great archangel. Of course, Jense has lots to say about that.

As the conversation tapers off, Yeshua rubs his hand across the wooden coffee table almost as if inspecting it, and I am reminded of the great builder that he is.

"You know, just as you are preparing for the Great Feast, Father and I are preparing for something as well." He looks up to see us listening closely, not wanting to miss what he is about to say. "The excitement that you all have now, I love, but I am ecstatic when I think of seeing your reaction to what we have been building for you. Some have seen a glimpse of the New Earth that is to come.

"What is it like, Lord?" asks Jense.

"You have read what the Holy Book says, Jense."

"Yes, but I want to hear it from you."

Yeshua folds his hands and smiles. The fine lines around his eyes become more prominent, and there seems to be a sparkle in his eyes that I didn't notice before. "It is new. Everything is new." He pauses for a moment as if to give us time to think about what he is saying, and then he continues. "Lands for discovery, untouched by anyone—can you imagine what sorts of hidden beauty you might find? Imagine because it is better than that."

We are like eager children sitting wide-eyed with wonder listening to grand stories. I can remember believing in Santa Claus and the excitement I'd have knowing that he was preparing gifts for me, and then the disappointment I felt when I realized it was only make-believe. But this is not a pretend fairy tale or make-believe. This is real. This is VERY real.

"And I will leave you with this," he says, sitting on the edge of his seat. "Our father, Elohim, he will no longer live in Alpha with the angels, separated from man. But he will live on the New Earth with all of you and with me. There will be peace and holy love, without fear, just as we have here. Except no mourning and no loss. Families will be together on land that is their own and houses that will never be taken away. There will be no need for guards, and unlike here the gates will always stay open, and the throne will be accessible and approachable by all. Every good and perfect gift, that is what we are preparing for you."

He lightly claps his hands on his knees, and then standing from the chair he concludes, "Now I must go, thank you for your hospitality."

He takes Grandma into his arms and kisses her cheek, and then embraces Gramps as anyone would an old friend. Jense and I walk him to the front door, and after our goodbyes we watch him walk out into the night, emitting only a warm glow. I'm left alone on the porch, watching him disappear so that it's only me and the crickets singing quiet songs of admiration.

I know my part now—with the Great Feast—and I am still baffled that he would pick me. From organza pouches to clothing for a king. But that is who he is, this God that I have come to know and deeply love. He is a builder in every sense of the word. Yes, a builder of objects but also a builder of man. And that is how I feel tonight—built up, and more importantly . . . *chosen*.

4. HUNTING

Leaves slap against my face, but it doesn't hurt. The enticing scent of dirt and pine needles call us deeper into the woods. The forest is pleasantly cool, and there is no sound of anyone else nearby. I look at Jense fully dressed in camouflage and holding a bow and arrow. I've never seen him this way before, but it suits him. I have also never hunted before, but I have target shot with sling shots quite a bit, so naturally that is what I decided to hunt with. Jense and I are staying clear of the bovine, leaving the slaughtering of cattle to those who are experienced. We walk at a mortal pace looking for any movement or indication of animal life. It wasn't hard to decide that I would be on the look out for the pheasants and he would hunt the bigger animals. We're not really sure what to expect though. Yeshua was very vague on details even though Jense pressed him for answers.

"I'm really surprised by how fun this is, sort of like a treasure hunt," I say, breaking the silence.

He looks at me and smiles, then returns to being the serious hunter. I find it amusing so I snicker. Without looking he grabs a handful of leaves from a branch sticking out in front of him and playfully throws them in my face. I laugh out loud, and then I quickly cover my mouth. There is a rustling ahead. Jense holds his hand out, and we both become completely still. Another rustle. He nods his head toward a nearby tree, and in a flash we are behind it. We quietly peek around it and watch. I think I see the head of an animal grazing. Yes, it is, and as it moves into view I can tell that it is definitely the ovine. Yeshua told us that it resembles a sheep but has the attitude of a ram. It does look like a sheep but with fur like a rabbit instead of wool and the color of light caramel. It is now in full view. Jense readies his bow and holds his arms steady. Just as he is ready to let go, the ovine jumps out of sight. Searching through the trees, we spot it again. It begins to run in a zig zag formation and now at a competitive speed. We could transport and catch up with it, but we just stand there watching as it joins a herd behind the boulders of large rock at the forest's clearing. This clearing connects to the base of the Holy Mountain, and unlike the mountain or the forest, it is rocky and desert- like. The animals have blended in so well to their surroundings, that even with our keen sense of sight we are unable to spot them.

"Should we go?" I ask Jense.

"Maybe behind that tree," he whispers.

"Let's climb it so we can have more of an advantage. While we're up there we can try to spot cervidae too, and maybe a pip or pose for me."

"That would be too easy, Coco."

"Oh—okay. What do you suggest?"

"Let's transport behind that tree to get a better look."

So we do. I know how much Jense wanted to do this, and I'm only here out of curiosity.

It's quiet, and we cannot see them anywhere. Animals in the Garden do not act this way. They never run away or hide because they have no fear of mankind. And though these ovine act as if they are mortal, I have a feeling they do not run or hide out of fear. Instead it seems more as if they are challenging us, making the catch more exciting.

We wait and still nothing. Jense walks out of the edge of the forest and onto the dusty ground at the base of the boulders, so I follow him. As we approach, nothing.

"Very strange," he says.

He slowly reaches out to touch the boulder, closer . . . closer . . . when suddenly an animal clucks, and the herd of ovine come running out of the rock itself and right through Jense and I. We stand there as the force passes through our now transparent bodies. Jense laughs and lets out a loud yell.

"Yeah!" he shouts, and laughs some more.

I can't help but laugh at him and this whole scene. A strange herd of animals running through our bodies—it's not something that happens every day.

The ovine make their way back into the woods, so we follow closely behind them and then beside them, running through leaves and over branches. Jense gets his bow ready, stops, and takes the shot. The arrow flies straight and precise, and with the force needed, it breaks into an ovine and takes it down to the ground. We stop abruptly as the rest of the herd continues on. Jense kneels at the side of the ovine and gently removes the arrow. He puts his hand over the wound, and when he removes it the wound is gone, but the animal remains lifeless.

"Well, that was unexpected . . . all of it," he says.

I smile at him.

Together Jense and I pick the animal up and transport to the plantation where some of our uncles are gathered at a table playing cards. Gramp's two brothers, Mike and Charlie, sit on a bench while their uncle, Clyde, and their great-uncle, Lewis, lounge directly across in their own chairs. They are all laughing at a move that Uncle Charlie made; then, like school children, they are gathered around us.

Lewis lets out a whistle.

"Well, would you look at this beauty," Uncle Mike says.

"I never seen a sheep with fur like this before," says Uncle Charlie.

"No siree," says Uncle Clyde. "We can make something real pretty with fur like this. You leave this pretty thing right here and we'll take care of it for ya."

"Thanks," we both say, and in an instant we are back in the forest at the place we left off.

"Do you wanna go find the animal that made that clucking noise?" Jense asks me.

"No, I think I'll live." He smiles at my figure of speech.

"I'm sure we will come across more as we go," he says.

"Yeah, and if not . . . seriously, I won't be heartbroken." Killing animals is not my favorite thing, and after watching Jense and the ovine, there's no telling what the pheasants will be like. "I mean, don't get me wrong, this is fun and all, I just think I should take a more supportive role and help you track."

"Okay," he smirks. "Then let's go deeper into the forest because I have a feeling that's where the cervidae will be."

Until now, we have been walking along the forest's edge with the Holy Mountain west of us. Now, we run into the heart of the forest where all that we see are trees and shadows. I say run, but it is more like spurts of flashes, making the expression "leaps and bounds" applicable—we run a little, transport ahead further, then run again, and transport again. Jense wants to go to the thickest parts where not even a ray of light shines through, but we are still surveying the area as we go. It is darker and cooler here but not uncomfortable to us. Again, Jense's hand goes out motioning me to stop. We hear talking.

Jense gives a friendly, "Hello?"

Two men stand from behind a tree and then are instantly in front of us. I recognize one of the men, Tommy, right away.

"Hi there, haven't met you two before," says the other.

"Uncle Paul, this is Jense and Coco," Tommy introduces.

"Oh?" He searches his thoughts. "John's grandkids?"

"Yes, sir."

"Well, I've been wanting to meet you two. Sorry I haven't sooner. I build with Tommy and John, and I've heard lots about you."

Tommy is Gramps' closest friend. He and Paul live on the western edge of our community with their families. Gramps says you can walk straight off of their land into the river that separates Epsilon from Delta. That is perfect for Tommy considering how much he enjoys fishing.

"Y'all probably know Tommy's two boys, Bradley and Scottie, sitting over there, huh?" asks Paul.

"Yes, sir, we've met," I say.

We wave to the twin boys and smile. They are young—I would guess seven or eight at death. Gramps never told us much about Tommy or his family, and we have only been around them a few times, but we know they are very special to him.

"Yeah, your grandpa and I go way back," says Tommy.

Paul nods his head. "Should've seen his face when Yeshua told him he was going to get you two. He was so proud of you both and so excited to have you in his house."

"Where is your grandpa?" asks Tommy. "I'm surprised he and Minnie didn't come hunting with the two of you."

"They already made plans to go to the beach today. It's sort of their thing. Grandma collects pearls, and Gramps looks for interesting shells for his furniture," I explain.

"Yeah, that's right. The two of them always loved the beach. We would take trips to Florida together."

"You mean you knew them as mortals?" I ask.

"Did I? Yes, we were friends for many years. Here, y'all come have a seat if you'd like, and I'll tell you all about it."

I look at Jense and he nods, so we sit down on the leaves next to Bradley and Scottie. I know Jense really wants to find a cervidae, but we are both interested in hearing a good story. Tommy's long, husky legs stretch out past ours as he and Paul take a seat next to us. His auburn mustache matches his hair, and his broad shoulders invade my space, but I don't mind it.

Tommy continues his story. "Yes, John and I played football together in high school. I went on to play professionally while John, as you know, opened his construction company building custom houses. We reconnected later on while I was living in California, and I asked him to come to Los Angeles and build me a house. It was a big house, and he did a fantastic job. They stayed for months, even rented a place, and it was very profitable for them in the end, *and me*—I got the house." He gives a quick laugh. "That's when your mom," he points to Jense, "Claire, fell in love with California. Nicole seemed to like it alright, but her heart was set on going to New York someday, and I believe she did, is that right, Coco?"

"Yes, that's right. But we moved to California several months before coming to the Garden."

"Okay. Well, your family was like family to us. I didn't come from a believing family, you see. Only Uncle Paul and our wives and children came to belief in Yeshua, which is why we're pretty much the only one's here from our family. We've got some very distant relatives here and there through the generations but none of our immediates. They were just non-believers—didn't believe in anything in particular. Thankfully, I got reconnected with your grandpa. My wife and I were going through some hard times . . . . ." He points his hands at his sons, and then he pauses for a moment. "We lost our boys here in a fire, see, leaving us and our two small daughters at the time. John and Minnie stood by us and walked us through. That's why we are here today. We had neighbors who were believers, and they shared good words with us, but John and Minnie . . . they walked it out with my wife and I, and we are eternally grateful to them."

Listening to Tommy speak of the impact that my grandparents had on his life makes me so proud of them. I often wonder what sorts of things I could do differently if I were to go back. Besides the obvious of sharing salvation with, *well*, everyone . . . knowing what I know now there would be a lot of changes. For one thing, my friendships would be different, that's for sure. The silly arguments that we would have . . . I just can't imagine that those *big* issues would even matter. The things that I love about friendship here is that there is no need to compete with anyone, and there's no putting down of anyone in order to feel better. What would my life had been like if I would have lived that way as a mortal? It was possible to prefer others there, I just hadn't had that lesson worked into my heart yet. I was so insecure, and all of the petty disappointments consumed so much of my time. Yep, so much would change. But I think above all, I would simply share hope. That is what Gramps and Grandma gave to Tommy and his wife. Their whole lives were changed because of it, and here they are today— in eternal life.

We are so busy talking, and me pondering, that we didn't even notice the large, black figure standing there looking at us with a fixed and curious stare.

"Cervidae." The words creep out of Jense's mouth.

No one wants to make any sudden movement so we sit for a moment and stare at the dark beast. It doesn't back down. He's a beautiful creature with the body of a large elk, but his coat is a shiny black, like a panther. His almost glowing, yellow eyes are entrancing to look at, and just like the ovine, I see no sign of fear. Instead of running away, he begins walking right toward us. We all look at each other confused, then watch him in stillness. This large, dark creature walks right up to us, bows his head, and to our astonishment . . . lies down before us. We are all in shock.

"He is giving his life to us," Tommy explains.

"I can't shoot him with an arrow," replies Jense, fumbling with his bow.

"Here, I have a knife," offers Paul. He hands him the knife, and Jense kneels at the cervidae's side. They look each other in the eyes, and the honorable creature gives an assuring look as if to say, "It's okay, this is my purpose."

Jense looks at the other men and they nod. He lifts the knife, and with a quick force he plunges it into the animals heart. It makes no sound but closes it's eyes and remains still. Jense removes the knife and again places his hand on the wound. As before, the wound is completely gone. We all kneel because for some reason it feels appropriate—like this is a holy moment—and, as Paul begins to lead us in praise to God, I understand why.

"Thank you, Yeshua, for giving your life as the ultimate sacrifice for us. You alone, Oh Lord, are worthy to be praised."

✦

It was an experience, that's for sure. Walking up to the

house, I look at Jense and his cervidae and wonder what his dad, my Uncle Brody, would say.

"I wish your dad would have been here for this," I tell him.

"My dad doesn't like to hunt, Coco—he's a surfer."

"*Oh*, he's a surfer, and surfers don't like hunting . . . like *you*?" I tease.

"You know what I mean. He's always been more of the *be one with the earth* type. Besides, he's a vegetarian."

"Well, either way I think he would have had fun with you today."

"Yeah, I guess he would have. What about your dad, do you think he hunts?"

The question takes me by surprise. "Hmm, I don't know. He's an artist *so* probably not."

I look up with a sly grin and see Jense's head tilted, his eyes enduring my sarcasm. He playfully steps on my foot, and my yelp alerts the others that we have arrived. Letty runs over, eyes large and mouth open.

"What is that?" she asks, jumping up to get a better look.

"It's called a cervidae," I tell her.

"Wow." She runs off and then disappears. My guess is that she is going to find Lion to tell him of the beast that he has to go and see.

"Thanks for today, Coco." Jense nudges me with his elbow.

"Hey, I'm glad you got your animals. Maybe next time I'll *git ma'self a pip*," I say in a southern accent.

"Next time? Really?" he asks.

"Um, . . . no. My hunting days are over."

"Well, mine might be too. Do you think we will hunt during the Millennium?"

"The Millennium? What's that?"

"You know, after the Great Feast . . . after the war?" he

responds quizzically. "The *Millennium*?" he asks again, expecting it to ring some sort of bell.

It's not hard for him to realize that I really don't know what he is talking about by the confused expression on my face.

"You don't know? Amraphel hasn't discussed this with you?"

By Amraphel, he is speaking of an angel who is also my teacher.

"No, he hasn't," I say. I haven't heard the term before, and I'm not sure what he means.

He tries to explain it to me. "It's a time of a thousand years where after the war we stay on mortal Earth and live with mortal man. Yeshua will be king there—on the earth that we know."

I understand what he's saying, but it's such a new idea for me to take in. "I guess I just assumed that after the war we would go right to the New Earth."

"Really?" he asks, but it's more of a way to state his disbelief. "Well, ask Amraphel tomorrow. He will explain."

"I will," I say.

Mortal Earth? How is all of this possible? I suddenly have so many questions to ask my teacher. Could immortals really live in a mortal land? Then answering my own question I realize, . . . *they already do.*

5. DAY ONE

It is Day One for Epsilon, which means that our entire community stops everything and journeys to Alpha, up to the Holy Mountain. Men, women, and children walk the path of that mountain on their first day of every week. Only Epsilon travels today because even though each community keeps to a weekly schedule of seven days, our days line up differently. For instance, when it is Day One here, it is a different day in the other communities. Another factor on Day One is that because there are over millions of people in each community we must go in groups of hundreds of thousands at different times throughout the day. Since we live furthest away from Alpha near the coast, our group goes first—right after the rooster's crow.

This morning, our family from the tea plantation gathered beforehand so that we could walk, *well*, transport together. We met up with neighbors as we appeared at the end of the wall of people waiting to get in. Now many have dispersed among the crowds, finding friends and making new ones, talking and catching up with one another.

I know that we are getting closer because both sides of the path are now lined with angels—their light radiating brighter than what we normally exhibit day to day. But as we walk between them, our colors begin to brighten too, and that brightest light now radiates through us. Jense and I touch each other with the same curiosity as last week and the weeks before. It never gets old poking him and seeing the light get dimmer where I touch.

"Hey, Letty, look! It's the rainbow!" I scoop Letty up in my arms, and Jense lifts Lion up on his shoulders. Looking above at the inclining path before us, there's an appearance of a rainbow from the colors of everyone's bodies now lit with the bright light. I can see the gates ahead as the rainbow becomes shorter from people entering Alpha. Because we cannot transport before Elohim's throne on our own, we must first go through the gates. Yeshua told us that in the New Earth we will be able to access the throne at any time, but right now, our access is still limited.

As we approach, the flowers and the rocks begin singing familiar songs of praise. We pause our conversations to sing out a line of the song being sung, but the closer we get, the quieter we become. A tall set of opened, double gates made of pure gold stand fixed before us, along with the two cherubim by the name of Aedhel and Durward who are keeping guard. Cherubim are a race all of their own, and they are giant—like fifteen feet giant. Instead of two wings they have four, with discreet eyes covering each wing. They have the ability to see completely around them at all times without having to turn their heads. I walk past them through the gates and enter the green courtyard that will lead into the City of Angels.

Fruit trees line the path, and I choose a red apple just as I always do and begin to eat. The people ahead of us move forward so that my feet come to the end of the path. I slowly step out of the courtyard and onto the golden cobblestones of the town square. This is where angels carry out their daily duties, but today they mingle with people. It is a cozy and enchanted town, almost like a historic downtown with shops and small markets. The markets carry angel food called manna and other types of airy wafers. It's not food that we humans chose to eat because there is no real flavor to them for our tongues. But for fun, we like to try the samples that are offered out on the countertops. I felt giddy the first time I tried any, fascinated with the idea that I was eating what Moses and the people of the book of Exodus survived on. The fact that it's angel food is enough to be enamored by.

The shops, on the other hand, are actually for us humans and are filled with electronic type items that the angels have made. Grandma's favorite find was a digital photo book with the shape of a thumbprint on the back. When in contact with a human thumb, it scans the person's mind and takes snapshots of images from their memory. This is how we enjoy photographs in the Garden. The frames hanging in our hallway work the same way and were found in one of these shops. It would be scary to have something like this in the hands of a mortal with all of the evil that could abound. Thankfully, mortal man is limited by their technological advancements.

As intriguing as the market and shops are, what really catches my attention the most is the large, cathedral-like building to the right—the Holy Library. It is white and glowing with the most glorious stained glass windows I have ever seen. It reminds me of the St. Louis Cathedral at Jackson Square in New Orleans. My mother took me there once when I was a child.

Jense interrupts my fond memory with a tug on my arm. "Come on," he excitedly nudges.

Following the golden cobblestone road up and through the clearing of the trees, in the distance our eyes can see the expanse of people gathered before the circular castle, kneeling on the green fields that lead up to it. There is still quite a distance before we can reach them, but now that we are past the gates we can transport again. Jense grabs my hand and leads me to an open spot where we kneel alongside of the others. Even with the multitudes that are gathered, there is still an expanse of empty land further than my eyes can see. We quietly wait and take time to ourselves to pray. It isn't very long before I hear the birds fly over and begin to sing. I open my eyes and look into the clear white sky around us. The few scattered clouds move and shift around until they form a large face—too large for anyone to overlook. As the clouds evaporate, Elohim's face appears to be as liquid.

"Rise," he says kindly, and we do.

It is interesting because he is looking right at me, but if you were to ask Jense he would say that he is looking right at him. And I know that for me right now, it's as if it is just he and I. Drum beats begin along with the strumming of guitars, and now violins join in with them. The angels begin appearing in the expanse of the sky surrounding the face of God and leading us in songs to him. "Holy, Holy, Holy, is the Lord God Almighty, who was, and is, and is to come," we sing. And now, in our own way, we begin to sing songs to him from our hearts. I feel him hugging me, even though when I look upon him I only see his kind eyes smiling at me.

"Thank You," I hear him say. "I love you."

His face gradually disappears, and I am again aware of the multitudes of people around me, but the feeling of his love stays. Lights begin to flicker in the now empty sky. Like a slideshow being projected, faces and scenes of people play out before us. "These are the redeemed," his voice sounds out from somewhere unseen, and the angels begin to cheer. It is infectious, and now we are all cheering and rejoicing over those whom have chosen to believe. Like a stadium of fans, we cheer for our team, but we are more than just fans —we are family, and we know what they now have to look forward to.

◆

Jense and I walk up the black, serendibite steps and enter the large, wooden doors. The smell of books mixed with lacquered wood confirms where we are. There is something about this library that arouses reverence—maybe because it is so ancient, or more probable the fact that it holds the very words of God on its shelves. I feel small walking across the wide, marbled path in the center; rows of tall bookshelves tower on both sides. At the end of each row there are tables and sitting areas—I wonder which one I will study at today. It is not bright like it is outside, even with all of the angelic teachers in the place. And though it is well lit, it is a warm and calming kind of light.

Jense immediately spots his teacher, Dominey, and gives me a squeeze on my arm. "See ya later," he says.

"Okay, see ya."

I scan the room for my teacher, Amraphel, until I see him standing and talking to another angel. They are both very tall—maybe seven feet—but not nearly as large as the cherubim at the gates. These angels are teachers full of the knowledge of the secrets of God and of his kingdom. Each are assigned to teach us the things that Elohim finds profitable for our future and for our life until then. In essence, they are preparing us for our destiny. Even now, we do not know exactly what our roles will be for eternity, and we will not find out until those books of the final judgment are opened at the end of all time. So, we wait in expectation and learn everything we can from our teachers. One incredible thing about being immortal is that our memory is restored to its full capacity, meaning that everything we learn and are taught we remember and do not forget.

Amraphel waves his hand at me and quickly ends his conversation with his friend. His curly hair is a mixture of blonde and light brown; his crystal blue eyes penetrate to the soul. He is wearing a long white robe, and there is a warm glow coming from his being, just like the other angels in the library. They are like lanterns, giving light but still keeping to the mood of their surroundings. We clasp hands and greet. His mannerisms are almost human but a little too exact to feel completely normal—like the way he precisely shakes my hand and stares straight into my eyes without blinking. It was a bit uncomfortable at first, but I've grown used to him now. He leads me down the marbled aisle until we come to row twenty-five. I glance at the books as we pass by, trying to read some of the titles, but there aren't any . . . only numbers. It feels like a long walk before getting to the end where a round, wooden table and two chairs of different sizes await us. He pulls a chair out for me first, and then his large body fills the taller chair next to it. On the table sits a thick, brown book with the word *Family* embroidered in golden, script font. Amraphel doesn't waste any time, but gets right to the teaching.

"Today, we will begin learning about your ancestors—the men and women before you and spoken of in the Holy Book. It is very important for you to know of these, and you did not learn it in your former life."

As interested as I am in hearing these stories, I have

questions and hope to get answers. My conversation with Jense yesterday has kept my mind reeling and wondering, and I don't want to wait another week before discussing our future life on Earth.

"I was actually wondering if we could discuss something, maybe a little different today?" I suggest.

He searches my face with his eyes. "Ah, the Millennium," he states.

"Yes."

He pauses for a few seconds. "As you wish," he says abruptly, closing the book and pushing it aside. He stares off to the right of me listening for something. I am guessing that he is communicating telepathically with someone because I have seen him do this before. "Ah, yes," he says.

Taking my hand into his—and totally unaware to me—we transport to a place of complete darkness. This I have not experienced since the time Yeshua carried me into the kingdom, with Jense and an angel at our side. Amraphel stands next to me as only an outline, and looking down I realize so am I.

"Where are we?" I ask, examining my body to see if I am still the same.

"You are okay," he says, touching my shoulder. Both of our bodies are now illuminate.

"We are between worlds. I'm going to show you something, but I need you to eat this first."

He hands me a pear. "A pear? Okay." I eat the fruit and study him. "I only meant for you to explain the Millennium to me. I wasn't really expecting to go there."

"We're not going there, and . . . this is more fun," he replies.

That seems like an odd choice of words coming from him. I'm not sure what Amraphel knows of fun. I've never seen an angel enjoying himself to that point before. They make friends and have community, but fun seems a little far-fetched.

"Fun for you or for me?" I ask him.

"Both," he replies, unconvincingly. "I rarely leave the Garden. This will be fun."

It's almost robotic which makes me laugh. "*Okay*—but it is a little frightening too," I admit.

"It's not frightening, you are with me," he says, smiling.

I do find solace in his words, and I'm suddenly at peace again. Was it the pear or the trust that I have for him? Probably both.

"We are waiting to pass, it shouldn't be too much longer."

"Waiting for what?" I ask.

"You are very inquisitive, aren't you?" He smiles and pats me on the back.

A larger creature fades into sight—an archangel—dressed just as Michael was at the wine harvest, except instead of a red cape, his is sapphire blue. He has dark skin, if that's what you'd call it, and on the top of his left hand is a small tattoo just above his wrist bone. It is a symbol—an X.

"You are all set," he assures us. I don't know what we are *all set* for, but like it or not I'm getting ready to find out.

"Thank you, Uriel," replies my teacher.

Again, Amraphel takes my hand, and it is pitch black for a good ten seconds until my eyes begin to focus and adjust to a new place and a new type of light.

It is a palace, I determine, and the man standing before me is dressed in a grey suit and talking to another suited man. They look European, Italian maybe, but I cannot hear their voices to make out their language. I watch them talk to one another, almost secretive even though they are alone in the large room.

I open my mouth to speak, but I am cut off.

"The one on the left, he is the man of lawlessness," Amraphel asserts, knowing what I was getting ready to ask.

"You mean the antichrist?"

"Yes."

"He is here? This is now?"

"Yes."

I curiously watch him. Both men are wearing a pin, a circular medal with a star symbol etched into it—some sort of insignia. In fact, looking around the room, this star symbol is on a lot of things. A flag standing upright behind the desk. The letterhead on the papers they are leaning over. A nearby photograph of what looks like world leaders, all wearing the medal star pin. My stomach drops and I say aloud what I'm thinking, "The mark of the beast . . . " The words drip from my tongue like slow honey. It's not that I've doubted the Holy Book, but to actually see these things come to pass this way is pretty profound.

"Do you know the definition of king, Coco?" asks Amraphel.

"Not the official one," I admit.

"A male sovereign or monarch who holds the chief authority over a country and people," he recites. "This man that you see imitates a king, just as his master, Satan, does. They both appear to be sovereign, to have all authority; one of course is physical and the other spiritual. They act as such and are followed as such. You and I both know who the rightful king is, though, do we not?"

"Yes."

"It is only a matter of time before this earthly rulership comes to an end—the blasphemies, the senseless killings, the injustice. That is the purpose of the Great War. But what do you suppose will happen to those left living on the earth?"

"Well, . . . they will continue to live, traumatized and in need of a lot of therapy."

He generously smiles. "They will continue to live under a new rule. A peaceful rule. That is the Millennium. A time when our king, the most holy, will be king on the earth."

"Do people know? Do my parents know? About this man I mean."

"They have suspicion."

"What about the mark? Did they refuse his mark?"

"Come, it is time to go now."

"Wait, why?"

He grabs my hand. "Now," he says sternly.

I'm not sure when it happened, but at some point everything went black.

"Coco," whispers an ethereal voice. I fight to open my eyes. "Coco." This time it's louder and clearer. His face, along with another angel, comes into view, and I adjust my eyes to their bright light. I can remember a commotion, and there are images . . . images of dark creatures in pursuit of us. Sometime between the passing from that world to my own I became weak and must have fainted.

"Amraphel . . . " I thinly mumble. "Were we in danger?"

"Of course not," he assures me, "It was only a disruption. Here, drink this."

Looking up at the high vaulted ceiling, I realize that I am back in the library. Amraphel lifts my head from the couch and brings a small bowl to my mouth.

"Was it really necessary?" asks the other angel.

"Yes, of course," he responds.

The warm liquid oozes down my throat. "Pea soup?" I ask.

"Not quite," he replies, cracking a smile.

Immediately my strength is regained, and the colors . . . the smells . . . everything is enhanced. I sit up and look around. "Can I take some of that soup with me for later?"

"She's inquisitive and funny," he responds, looking over at the other angel who seems to still be inquiring about something I don't understand.

"Wait, did you knock me out or something?"

"I only put you to sleep for a short time and now you are awake. I'm sure you have many questions, and I would be happy to address them the next time that we are together, but for now your cousin awaits you."

Somehow squinting my eyes is the natural reaction to my current wondering. I've realized there's not a whole lot of reasoning with an angel. They receive and give orders, that's what they do.

"Okay." I stand up expecting to be weak, but I'm not—I feel fully recovered. "Thank you for taking me today and showing me. I hope your time out of the Garden was fun."

"Yes," he says with a nod.

I walk slowly back through row twenty-five and take a right turn down the marbled aisle. If I thought I had questions before, this only sparked my curiosity more. So far I know two things. First, I know that *the* antichrist is on the earth, the one that was prophesied about in the Holy Book. It doesn't seem like anyone realizes who he is yet though. I try to figure out a timeline in my head, but for me it would only be speculation because I haven't been taught about it, and from what I've read I'm just not sure. Second, I know, or at least I think I know, that the Gathering has to happen soon because we are already preparing for the Great Feast.

"Bah!" yells a voice as someone jumps towards me. I am startled from my thoughts, and I stumble backwards.

"Jense!"

"You should see your face!" he says, laughing.

"Be quiet, we're in a library," I whisper back.

That seems to make him laugh even harder. I grab his arm, and we run out of the large wooden doors—Jense laughing like a child, and me trying not to look amused . . . but I can't help it. It was funny. So funny that I am buckled over laughing—hysterically.

"It's not that funny," Jense says between gasps.

"I think it's the soup," I manage to get out.

"What?" He is confused and rightly so. "When does anyone have soup in a library?"

I try to compose myself. "Today, I guess."

6. FIT FOR A KING

The overstuffed, down-filled couch feels perfect right now. I'm like a rabbit, biting on the end of my pencil—it's what I do when I'm thinking creatively. Staring at a blank stack of paper, I do feel inspired, but I'm still unsure. When I close my eyes I can see Yeshua clearly in my memory. His robe has to be perfect—something fit for a king, but also warrior-like. A picture comes to my mind and I begin to sketch, but to no avail.

I'm thinking samurai will be the influence for the robe. I am pleased with the idea, but I need to take a trip to our community library to see pictures. It should be less eventful at this library—no transporting to mortal land or time, and no fainting or strange soups.

It is tending day today, so everyone is busy with their responsibilities. I would usually make pouches, but Grandma suggested that I use tending days to work on the garment, and Yeshua agreed that it was a good idea. I have extra made anyway, so it should be enough for a week or maybe two. I'm not sure how long it will take me to make the garment, especially considering I've never done anything like this before.

I don't really want to go to the library alone, but Jense is surfing with friends and when he gets back he'll dry tea. *Maybe Leslie would go with me.*

I gather my papers and run up the stairs to my room to get a bag to carry them in. A cotton shoulder bag hangs on a hook behind my door. *Perfect.* I change my appearance from the velvet house clothes to a simple, light-blue dress—a similar blue to the color of my walls. Sitting on a stool in front of the full length mirror, I brush my long hair and braid it. My eyes are drawn away to the reflection of the painting above my bed. It's a beach scene that even I was surprised that I could paint. I started taking a real interest in painting when we moved to California, but I was very amateur. Here, it comes natural—something just clicks and makes sense. It's like I've painted all of my life.

"Meow." Lansing is all curled up on my window seat of yellow and white pinstripe fabric, sandwiched between two floral pillows which match the set on my bed. I can't resist picking him up; his long, white fur is so soft against my face. Rubbing my nose on his head, I give him a kiss. He smells like clean cotton or better yet, fresh laundry.

"Goodbye, Lansing," I sing as I lay him back down in the same comfy spot.

The warmth of outside feels so good. It's a beautiful day as always—birds are singing, and flowers are in full bloom.

Gramp's sister, my Aunt Tildie, loves gardening, so she tends to the flowers at our house and hers. She sits at a multi-colored rose bush of white, pink, and yellow with a glass vase and pruners in her hands. Bougainvilleas and azaleas fill in the spaces behind it. Aunt Tildie is a true southern lady, and I love hearing her talk.

"Hi, Aunt Tildie," I say as I pass.

"Well, hey, baby. Come here." She takes her pruners and cuts a pink rose from the bush, then hands it to me. Immediately a sprout comes forth from the place where she cut, and a rose bud is already there.

"Thank you." I smell the rose, which is too sweet for words. "Can you put it in my hair?" I ask, turning around and squatting down in front of her.

"Suuure," she draws out, then sticks it in my braid at the base of my head. "A pretty rose for a pretty girl."

I give her a kiss on the cheek. "I'm going to the beach. I'll bring you back some orchids and wild roses."

"Oh, that would be so nice."

"See ya later."

"Bye-bye, sugar."

I decide to run because I like the way it feels. I don't get tired or out of breath like I would as a mortal. That was something that I despised before, but now it makes me feel energized and full of life. I hold my bag close to my vibrant blue dress. I can feel the rose stem gently poking my neck, reminding me that it's there, but I'm not worried about it because flowers in the Garden are hardy and do not lose their petals easily.

I pass the neighboring land and see Abby with her cousin, Pearl, riding horses in an open field and laughing. They notice me and lift their hands.

"Coco!" They shout and wave.

"Hey Abs, . . . Pearl!" I shout back. I called Abby "Abs" once and it became my nickname for her. Jense, being the jokester that he is, decided he would call her "Abs of Steel." She thinks it's funny.

Abby's family trains animals. I would've invited her to go today, but I heard they got those two new horses, so I knew she would be busy with that. Apparently even resurrected animals need to be taught and trained. Leslie's family are weavers and potters. They make baskets and pottery, and, of course, she makes her pretty hats. I'm hoping that maybe she can take time away from it today.

The square, white house is nestled between groups of palm trees and lush greenery. I run around to the back and find Leslie sitting on a blue and white striped lounge chair on the sand, and I can hear the peaceful sounds of the waves hitting against the shore. She has a set of white plates on a short table in front of her and a paint brush in her hand. I put my hands over her eyes, and she lets out her girly laugh and pulls my hands off.

"Coco! What are you doing here?"

"Just wanted to see if you could go to the library with me . . . I need to look for a book."

"Really, what kind of book?"

Her mother must have seen me coming because she opens the sliding glass doors with two drinks in her hands. There's even little umbrellas in them.

"I thought you girls would like some fresh lemonade."

"Thank you, that's perfect," I say.

"Mom, Coco, is on her way to the library and wanted to see if I could go with her, but I'm thinking we may have something here."

"What type of book are you looking for? Greg has a huge selection inside."

"I'm needing an illustrated book with photographs or pictures of Samurai."

"Well, you came to the right place. I'm sure we have something like that."

"Really? That's great. Would it be okay to borrow?"

"Yes, definitely. I'll go get it for ya."

"Thank you so much." *Wow. Score.* That'll save me a lot of time.

I watch Leslie paint a pattern of silver on the white plates.

"What are you painting, Les?"

"It's a pattern my great-grandmother created for a new set of plates. It's really pretty, isn't it?"

"Yes, it is," I say, admiring her talent. "So have you spoken to Yeshua about helping with the table settings?"

"I did!" She is clearly excited. "And, yes, I can help with it! In fact, our family is making the dinnerware for it."

"Wow, is this what it will look like?"

"Yes," she says, looking up from her painting job with a huge smile. "Oh, looks like mom found the book."

Meg returns with a hardback book titled, "The Truth About War." It is authored by Lou Ingram who lives in a cottage near Alpha. Sometimes on Day One we pass his house, and every time that we do I find myself studying the sculptures that are intentionally placed throughout his yard. There is an armored knight hidden within a large bush against his house. All that you can see is the head and chest, the feet sticking out at the bottom of the bush, and a sword in upright position being held by a hidden arm. My favorite is a sculpture of a little painted bird of orange and gray that sits atop a bird bath. Grandma told me it's a kakerori—a warrior bird. There is a common story that is told to the children here of a brave kakerori bird who fights a rat to the death in order to protect her children. I first heard the story on a camping trip with Gramps, Grandma, Jense and the kids from his surfing group. We were sitting around a bonfire, and Gramps told us the well known story. Then he proceeded to explain about the upcoming war that is going to take place. He explained how Yeshua and all of the men

of the Garden will fight for the eternal protection of the
Lord's children, and how evil will be no more. The boys, of
course, stood and engaged in a pretend sword fight while
the girls sat enamored at the idea of Yeshua and the men
fighting for them. Every time I see that sculptured bird I
think of that brave mother bird, and I am reminded of our
Lord's strong love for us.

"Here ya go," says Meg, handing me the book. "You
borrow it as long as you need to."

"Thank you!" I quickly thumb through the pages. "I can't
wait to be inspired." I give her a hug and then I kiss Leslie
on the cheek. "I'll see you soon, Les."

"Okay, Coco. I'm glad you came by."

"Me too. This saves me a trip to the library. Now I can get
home and back to work."

We say our goodbyes, and I decide to transport back, but
first I stop to pick some flowers for Aunt Tildie. As I make
my appearance near the couch, I hear children laughing
outside. Through the lace curtain, I see Lion and Letty
running around in the yard. I tap the window and wave,
and they wave back. Their sweet voices yell my name. "Hi,
Coco!" I hear from behind the glass. They take off running
again, and Lion jumps into Jense's arms. From the looks of
it, he is just now returning from surfing. That's good news
for me because it means I still have time while they are
tending to the tea.

I arrange the flowers in a glass vase and decide to give
them to Aunt Tildie later on. Pulling the book out of my bag,
I plop back down on the overstuffed couch, opening to the
Preface where Lou tells of his time with the angel Rayhem.
He explains that the knowledge and pictures shared in this
book are compilations of all that he learned from the angel. I
flip through the next few pages of writing and open to a full
page photograph. It is a man clad in an iron-like robe and
head gear, not really what I had in mind. I turn the pages to

more writing and funny looking illustrations of men in full, wide robes of oriental design. I'm starting to question whether or not this is the right book, when I turn the page and the image almost jumps out at me. *This is it.*

The photograph is of a man dressed just as I was picturing in my mind. He is wearing a kimono that is secured at the waist with pants underneath that open halfway down the leg and end above the ankle. That is not the part that impresses me, but the vest over the top does. It is a sleeveless, long vest with winged shoulders. Under the photograph is a caption that reads, *Twelfth Century Daimyo.*

This is exactly what I was looking for. I begin to sketch making modifications to all of it. I draw regular pants and a fitted shirt for sort of a base. For the robe, I use the vest as inspiration and sketch more of a sleeveless cloak, keeping the winged shoulders. *Perfect.* Hari should have the fabric I'll need, but now I'll have to wait until market.

◆

Jense and I walk through the crowds of people, most of them trading and sharing while others are in clusters here and there, talking and laughing. He is leading Dolly who follows closely behind us. The sun is warm on my bare shoulders; my long dress blows in the gentle wind. Jense says I look bohemian today. I tell him he looks platonic.

"Platonic? How do you mean?" he asks.

"Well, sort of beautiful really."

He lets out a short laugh. "Coco, I'm not following you."

"Your spirit is beautiful, Jense, that's all I mean."

"Well, thank you." He smiles his boyish grin. "I think you just wanted to use a big word though."

I shake my head and sigh. "Oh Jense, you are something."

"More compliments? Wow—must be my birthday."

I snort and give him a pat on the cheek. "You're *killing* me with your jokes."

"Ah, nice one."

I can remember going to school with Jense on my first day. It was obvious that the girls found him very attractive by the way they swooned to him and followed him around. Every girl that I knew wanted to date Jense Reed, the champion surfer. I often wondered if that was the only reason they were friends with me in the first place. And even though he still carries those same physical traits, it's not what's attractive about him here. I guess we all sort of have a platonic love so to speak.

"Hey, I'm gonna stop and talk to Hari, okay?"

"Sure, I'll take Dolly and set up."

Hari's tent is flowy but thick enough to block visibility of what's inside. I don't see him anywhere, so I browse his selections—paying specific attention to everything white. Along the three draped walls are shelves of fabrics, some on rolls, and others are hung near the top of the tent so that they delicately fall to the floor.

"Coco! I've been expecting you," a lively voice calls in a thick Indian accent.

I turn to see Hari with his arms open to me. "Come," he says, and walks to a wooden trunk in the corner of his tent. He opens the box and pulls out a solid white fabric, neatly pressed and folded.

"Yeshua told me you would be coming for it. We designed this type of linen ourselves."

"It's really beautiful, Hari."

"And it's wrinkle-free. Here, try to wrinkle it," he says, handing it over.

"I believe you," I laugh.

The special linen is smooth and such a clean, vibrant white. My creativity is stirring, and I see no reason why I should wait to get started. *I better let Jense know.*

"Thank you—I must go now."

He agrees and kisses my cheek. Within the time it takes to blink, I vanish and begin to appear before Jense and Sam who are sitting and talking behind the table of tea leaves.

"I'm going back to the house, okay?" I interrupt.

Jense seems to understand and nods. "Alright, see ya later."

"See ya."

I've always loved gardenias and their undeniable fragrance. I smell them now as I transition from the market to my bedroom. I'm not surprised to see them delicately placed in a small bowl of water on my nightstand—Grandma's doing. She also left a sewing book for me to study and the pattern that she and I worked on together. It doesn't take me long to gather the information that I need in order to begin.

Cutting through the fabric is a bit unnerving, but the more that I cut the more confident I become. I work through the evening, with precision and ability that I didn't know I had—sort of like when I'm painting. It's natural, and somehow I just know what I'm doing.

Laughter travels into my room from downstairs, pulling me out of my concentration, and I am thankful for the break of silence. From the sounds of it I would guess that Gramps, Grandma, and Jense are playing board games, and I'm pretty sure that I hear Sam too. I wouldn't normally pass up playing with them, but I'm in a zone—which isn't something I experience regularly, so I figure I better go with it.

"Hey, Coco!" I clearly hear Jense's voice calling through the cracked door. "You're really missing out!" he yells from below. I smile.

"You should be glad—you know I'd win!" I tease back. Everyone, except Sam, knows that I don't win very often.

"Oh, maybe you should stay up there then," yells Sam. I hear them mumble something and then continue with their game.

I do stay—all night, in fact, and through the morning. I can hardly believe it as I make my last stitch and finally finish the garment.

Laying it aside, I open and close my hands a few times and shake them from their monotony, then collapse on my bed with relief. I must say I am very pleased, and thankfully I am immortal because I'm not even a little tired. That nap I took the night of Day One may have helped. I've learned that I can go days without sleeping, and when I do sleep it's usually never longer than a few hours. I should be good for another day or two at least. I take a moment and stare at the ceiling. *Thank you.*

Water runs in the kitchen and footsteps walk across the floor below. Grandma's loud voice is resonating from downstairs. I stretch, then push myself up—ready for a change of scenery and communication with other human beings. I hang the robe and admire it one last time. Lansing's soft fur rubs against my leg.

"What do you think about the robe?" I ask, picking him up into a cuddle. His purr vibrates against my chest. "Oh, you like it too?" He paws at my shoulder. "What, you want to go join the rest of the family?" I ask in a silly, baby voice. The unresponsive cat just looks at me blinking.

From the top of the stairs I call down to my family, "Who's ready for competition now?"

7. FUN

The warm water touches my leg at the exact time that a seagull squawks. I open my eyes and see Jense, two young boys, and a girl on their boards riding a profound wave. The rest of the children are sitting at the water's edge, near me, watching and playing in the sand. I was talking to the Lord, just thanking him for the warmth and the peace. I have an aunt—actually she's Grandma's aunt—who lives with her husband's family in the community called Zeta. They have a rocky coast there, and the water stays cool. I prefer the warmer waters and the sandy beach of Epsilon, but I do like our trips to see them. Unlike here, they get snow on occasion, and that's usually the time when we make our visit. Their large log cabin is nestled in a forest at the base of a mountain range, with fireplaces in every room. The temperature stays comfortable during the day, but it can get cold there at night during the snowy times. I have great memories of snuggling up with Grandma in front of their fireplace and listening to their stories. It's like going to a cozy winter resort for a few days, then coming back home to summer—just the way I like it.

Little shots of water hit my face, taking me out of my daydream. Carlos is holding a small water gun and smiling at me playfully. I reach under my blanket and pull out a water gun that I stashed earlier from a boy named Ko.

"Oh yeah?" Carlos says, shooting at me. "*¡Toma!*"

Naturally, a water gun fight breaks out between us, and the other kids start jumping up and down, shrilling with excitement. I chase him into the water, and the waves overtake us. He is still trying to shoot me under the water. We come up laughing and I splash at his face, then grab his head and gently shake it. These kids are like the brothers and sisters I never had. Jense has an older sister who is married, but because she is older, he had felt like an only child most of his earthly life. Here, we all have each other, and even distance cannot separate us.

A hand grabs my foot, and before I realize it I'm pulled under. It's not surprising to see my cousin with a crooked grin. *Follow me*, I hear his thoughts.

We swim side by side passing white anemone and groups of starfish; bright blue fish are skimming the ocean floor below us. Angelfish swim by, and one brushes against my arm as if to say "hello."

Where are we going? I ask.

I found something, right over there.

We swim up to a coral reef, and as we get closer I can see what looks like open clam shells showcasing something special inside—pearls maybe. We are treading water above them now, and yes, they are clams with pearls—large pearls with a swirly pattern of pink and white.

Grandma?

Jense nods. He takes my hand to show me a beautiful necklace from his imagination. We grab only enough to make the necklace, then we swim back to shore. Surfacing, I lift one to get a better look.

"She's gonna love it," I say aloud.

"Yeah, let's get back."

Jense rounds up all of the kids, and we head back to the community center where we met up this morning.

The sound of balls hitting against bowling pins crack as we enter the attached Union building. On either side of the bowling alley there are glass windows; to the left is the roller skating rink and to the right are the ice skaters. The ceiling is also made of windows so that light can shine in. The kids are excited to run off and play, so Jense and I say goodbye and make our way through the pool tables and back outside.

"Do you hear that?" I ask him.

"Yeah, look over there."

In the distance, we can see the top of a ferris wheel peeking up above the trees. There is a carnival set up for tonight in the same field where we met for the wine harvest. A traveling group of carnies and circus performers circulate —going from one community to the next—setting up rides, games, and even a big tent where the performers and animals put on their spectacular show. Jense and I are going, but I plan on meeting up with Leslie there and spending the night with her afterwards. Knowing Les, she probably has lots of creative things planned for us to do. I'm sure we will make something, and we will probably go for a night swim in the ocean. It's one of my favorite things when I stay at her house. I can't wait to show her the pearls that Jense and I found today. Which reminds me that I still have my beach bag with the pearls in them for Grandma.

"Jense, let's bring this stuff home before we go to the carnival."

"Okay, I was thinking we'd go this evening anyway."

"Yeah, I'd like to go when everything is lit up, plus Gramps said that the circus performance is bigger at night with more animals."

We've only been to one previous carnival, and it was soon after we arrived in the Garden. Jense and I were so new to everything, so it was a great opportunity to meet people and make friends. In fact, that is how I met Leslie.

Gramps and Grandma are sitting on the porch swing drinking sweet, iced tea.

"Well, hey, y'all." I love that Grandma picked up a Louisiana accent to go with her already thick French one.

"How were the waves today?" asks Gramps.

"Noticeably larger than the last time we went," Jense animately replies.

"Is that right? I bet the kids had fun with that."

"And me," he says, running his fingers through his beached hair. "Coco, let me see your bag, please. We found something for you, Grandma. I'm gonna to make you something real special."

"Well, that is so sweet!"

Jense pulls out a pearl, and Grandma takes in a loud breath.

"Oh, that's so beautiful!" she says. "I've never seen any like this. Have you, John?"

"No, . . . that is something real special, isn't it?"

They rub their fingers over the smooth surface. "After all our beach trips I can't believe we haven't come across any before," says Grandma.

"Yep, it's amazing how many new things we continually find here. Just think of all of the things that are still undiscovered," says Gramps with a glimmer in his eyes.

Gramps loves a good discovery, and the Garden is a perfect place for it. I think that's why he and Grandma enjoy living close to the ocean and the mountains. There's lots of variety in what they find.

A small beeping goes off from inside.

"Oh, I forgot my biscuits. I can't wait to see what you make me, *bébé*." Grandma goes inside with Gramps carrying his glass in behind her.

"Co, I'm gonna go put these things away. I'll meet up with you a little later."

"Kay."

I wait on the porch steps, and the black birds begin to sing; the sun is bidding farewell for the day. Jense comes out in jeans and a white t-shirt, and I'm realizing that we match.

"You have good taste," I say, motioning to our clothes.

His white shirt changes to navy blue.

"Hey, don't you want to match me?" I ask.

Jense lifts one side of his face into an awkward side smile. "Eh, I like to be my own person."

"Okay, Mr. Unique . . . well, ask Grandma if they're coming."

He opens the screen door and pokes his head in. "Are you guys coming with us?" he yells.

"We're right here," Grandma says, coming to the door with Gramps standing over her shoulder.

"Oh, sorry," Jense returns.

Grandma pats his cheek. "We'll come in a bit. I wouldn't pass up a good funnel cake or a circus. And I know Gramps wants to ride a few rides, don't you?" She elbows him a couple of times.

"You know it!" he answers.

"Well, maybe we'll see you there," I say.

Jumping on Jense's back, I give a loud, "Yaw!" He carries me through the woods, and we can hear the music and the sounds of excited people in the distance. As we get closer, the upbeat tempo gets louder, and I can feel the bass thumping in my chest. It's no surprise when we reach the clearing and see a grand spectacle before us. It looks very similar to the state fairs I have gone to on earth—only cleaner and much bigger—with rides brightly lit by colorful bulbs, refreshment stands, and a large plethora of games to choose from. Straight ahead past the carnival, stands the big top with hundreds of balloons strung out and around it. There are no ticket stands, of course, because everything is free.

I look around for Leslie, but I only see smiling faces of game operators and their attendants. We agreed to meet at the ferris wheel, so that's where Jense and I decide to go first.

"Coco! Jense!"

I look up and see Leslie at the top of the ride, quickly on her way back down. A man wearing a name tag with *Jerry* etched into it, stands at the operating station with a big smile.

"Come join the fun," he says, and opens up the gate to the bucket where Leslie is sitting. Her sleeveless plaid shirt is tucked into high waisted, rolled up jeans.

We get in and hold on because even though it is going slow right now, we know the pace is about to pick up. Faster and faster the ferris wheel accelerates until all that can be seen of us are flashes of color to onlookers. We are laughing so hard and grabbing each other's arms with one hand and the poles with the other. A couple of kids hoop and holler from below us, and now their yells get further and further away. We go a few more rounds, then the ferris wheel begins to slow down. Jerry comes into view as I look below, and he is laughing and pointing out toward an open field a few hundred yards away. From the top we can see that the boys who were riding below us were thrown from their basket, and judging from their high five-ing I'm guessing it was intentional on their part. They transport back to their seat, and we hear them talking about how awesome that was.

"That was exhilarating, wasn't it?" Leslie asks, pulling back her hair into a ponytail.

"So fun!" I say, while Jense nods—still laughing.

We get out of the bucket, and Leslie and I grab hands to take off to another ride. Jense waves to a group of boys our age. "Maybe I'll see you girls at the circus," he says, walking in their direction.

"Okay!" we yell, meeting up with our own group of friends.

✦

I have been to earthly circuses where the lines are long and everything is overly priced. I have watched great performances from limited bodies, and I have taken seats next to people with rude and selfish attitudes. I am guilty of exhibiting those behaviors as well. Sitting here next to Leslie and the other girls, I close my eyes and realize how blessed I am. Roasted peanuts and the giggles of children fill my soul.

"Coco!" I hear from some very small, familiar voices. I open my eyes to see Lion and Letty running towards me with cotton candy in their hands.

"Hey guys! Oooh, cotton candy—yum!"

"Taste mine," says Letty, pulling the pink fluff and putting it to my mouth.

"Mine too," insists Lion. "I have blue."

The cotton candy melts on my tongue; its sweetness fills my mouth and rises so that I smell its sugary flavor.

"Ummm, thank you."

Leslie scoots over and pats the bench on the open space

between us.

"Come sit with us," she offers.

They look behind us at Christy with inquiry, and she nods her head.

"I'll be with Grandma over there." She points at Aunt Tildie who is sitting next to Gigi and Aunt Noemi. We wave at each other, and then Letty's little arm wraps around mine, and she and Lion scoot in between Leslie and I.

"What do you think is in that box on stage?" asks Leslie.

"Maybe—" I couldn't finish my thought because at that moment the brightly wrapped box in the center of the circular stage bursts open with the sound of a loud bang, making us all jump in our seats. Shiny, silver confetti rain down in center stage, and masses of balloons begin floating up around it from hidden places in the floor until all we can see above us at the top of the tent are balloons. We all clap and cheer. Letty looks up at me with a huge smile and excited eyes, while Lion is opening his eyes wide at us. He laughs and Letty starts to giggle. Loud roaring steals our attention.

"Lions!" I say, reaching over and putting my hand on Lion's back. A wide smile crosses his face. He searches until he sees them and makes sure that we do too.

Walking down the aisles are four lions with women dressed in long, flowy white dresses standing on top of each one. Their arms are out straight to their sides with their hands in fists. In unison, the women sit on the lions as they jump on stage. Pulling their closed hands to their mouths, they open them and blow what looks like red glitter. The lions each let out a big breath, and the already settled silver confetti rises into the air and mixes in with the glittery red, clearing off of the stage and into the crowds. Screams and laughter ring out from the children, and little hands everywhere are trying to grab the confetti. Trumpets begin to play as the lions with the women bow. Yeshua stands in the box seat that is straight across from us, holding his hand up in a wave and giving a winsome smile.

"Behold, the Lion of the tribe of Judah!" announces a loud voice. We all cheer and echo the announcer. *"The Lion of the tribe of Judah!"* we shout.

"That's my name," informs Lion, laughing to himself in the midst of all of the noise.

"That's right," we tell him, messing up his hair.

Cymbals clash and the trumpets make their last blast. Yeshua takes a seat next to three men dressed in similar clothing as he—white, light-weight tunics and dark pants. It's Peter, James, and John. I have never met them, but I have seen them with Yeshua before. Jense met Peter once during one of his study times with Dominey. He didn't tell me much about it though, only that he met his family. Jense said that Peter's wife introduced herself by the name "Pet." Peter told him it was a joke because her name was never mentioned in the Holy Book, and there was speculation on earth that her name could be Perpetua. It is known that his wife has a dry sense of humor. She is not here today, but it's probably because they live in Beta and already had their carnival. Besides, it isn't unusual for Yeshua to travel with his friends as he did as a mortal. Everyone knows of their bond, and everyone respects it.

The lights begin to dim, and people settle back into their seats and become quiet. Colorfully lit ramps rise onto the stage from below. In five random spots, men on unicycles rise up onto the stage and simultaneously ride up the ramps, do a flip and then land. Again and again they go, and each time the flips increase in number and in height. One more time they make their jump from the ramps, complete six flips, and just before landing they disappear—unicycles and all. Even though we know that they transported, we still clap and cheer because it was unexpected.

Letty points high above the stage as ten women are lowered holding onto sheer fabric strips. Suddenly ten more fabric strips fall at once in between each woman, and men instantly appear hanging onto the fabric. They take turns spinning and flipping in the air and latching back on to the sheer fabric that is now lit and glowing different colors. The men and women jump in the air out toward the crowds, vanish, and up jump monkeys from off of the stage taking their place on the fabric strips. People are pointing, and the children are clapping—some jump up and down, and others are laughing. The monkeys swing and jump from strip to strip. Some just hang and give ear to ear grins. Even Yeshua finds it amusing.

The performances only get better. Exotic cats put on a show with their tails. Horses and their costumed riders take the stage with elephants, and then bears. The riders lead them in tricks of all sorts. There are flying peacocks, comedian parrots, and small children on tight ropes. I love the fact that I have been shouting and cheering and my throat is not even sore.

As the show comes to a close, the big top slowly opens from above, and all of the gathered balloons lift up into the air. We look up to the now open sky full of stars and ascending balloons. Pops and bangs begin sounding off as colors burst into the sky taking the form of shapes and even animals. It's a fireworks display like no other I've seen before. The colorful lights appear to fall and then disappear before making it back into the tent. All of the performers take the stage and give their bows. We applaud and cheer loudly, and following Yeshua's lead, we give a standing ovation.

In a matter of minutes, the animals lower beneath the stage until they are no longer seen, and the performers disappear. You can hear the instant chatter as people talk about their favorite parts. Lion and Letty run excitedly to

Christy, retelling about the peacock that flew right above our heads.

✦

Leslie and I take hands and run down the lantern lit path. Clusters of wisteria hang down above us, and we take turns jumping to grab handfuls of the flowers. We stick them in our hair and playfully hit each other in the face with them.

"Let's go to the beach," Leslie says.

"You must've read my mind."

I transport to our favorite spot where the water calmly sits between tall walls of rocks, and I wait for Les. I now see that she transported under the water, and I laugh at such a clever idea and dive right in. It is so brightly lit that I can see everything clearly. The fish are very playful at night, swimming laps around us—some form tunnels for us to swim through. We come to a set of large rock formations that stick out of the water, and we climb on top and lay up against them. It is quiet in this moment—only Les and I looking out at our home from the vast waters. We can see the distant lights from her house back on land and the dim, lantern lights scattered throughout the woods. Looking further, my eyes follow the paths of lights that climb their way up the Holy Mountain and stop at the shielding cloud formation which brings us our night.

We both sigh as we take it all in.

"This is heaven," I say, resting my head back against the rock.

Les looks at me and smiles. "Yeah," she says.

8. MAJESTY

Rest. It's a gift, and we take advantage of it every Day Seven. I spread myself out on the cream-colored chaise as a knock comes to the door. Gramps and Jense turn their heads from their slouched positions on the couch.

"Well, who could that be?" Grandma wonders aloud from the kitchen. She wisps to the door, and we all notice the light flooding in from the crack below. "I think it's an angel," she says.

We sit up straight, waiting to see which angel has come to pay us a visit. It could be Amraphel or maybe one of the other teachers.

The door opens and we are speechless. He is even more

beautiful up close. Now that I think about it, I've never been this close to him before. The only archangel that I've personally been in contact with was Uriel, just this past week.

"Gabriel," whispers Jense.

Grandma turns to face me, "Coco, he is here to speak with you."

I scurry to the door and imagine tiny people playing drums on my heart—if I actually had one—because that is what it feels like. The messages that Gabriel brings are straight from the throne and mostly given to mortals—what could he possibly need to tell me?

I approach and for a second get lost in his captivating gaze.

"Coco, the Lord requests your presence today, and he wants you to bring the garment."

Oh, right—the robe. Wait, does this mean I get to go to the palace? . . . today? . . . on my own?

"Yes, I will come right away." I reply.

"He will meet you at the City of Angels and from there escort you to the palace."

"Thank you."

He gives me a simple nod, and then he is gone. I run to Grandma and grab her hands.

"It's time to bring the robe," I tell her in a rush.

"He will love it, *ma chèrie!*" she convincingly responds.

I bite my lip and smile. We both know that Elohim has already seen the robe. He is all knowing. But what does he think, and what will Yeshua think about it?

She gives my hand a good squeeze. "Go."

I run upstairs to my room. If I were a mortal right now I would be gnawing my fingernails, but I'm not, and instead of feeling anxious or worried, I feel excited. I have never been to the Holy Mountain alone before. *What should I wear?* It needs to be something special, so standing in front of my full length mirror I change my appearance to a long white gown. Grandma leans against my doorway. "Be yourself, that's what he will like."

She is right. I change from the white gown into a simple yellow dress. Looking at my milky skin, I admire how perfect my complexion is. I was just beginning to wear makeup as a mortal in order to hide some of the blemishes. No acne here. Everyone has the appearance of flawless skin.

"Can I do your hair?" Grandma offers.

"Yes, please . . . that would be great."

She runs the brush through, then pulls up half of my golden hair and creates a rope-like braid in the back.

"Thank you, Grandma." I give her a kiss on the cheek, then grab the garment hanging from a hook on the nearby wall. Gramps made the hooks for me out of old door knobs that he traded for at the market. Since I don't have a closet, they work perfect for hanging my bags and the hat that Les made for me.

"Well, here I go. See ya tonight, I guess."

"Okay, *bébé*. Have fun, darlin'."

We hug, then instantly I am at the gates. Standing about nine and a half feet taller than me are Aedhel and Durward. Without a word, they open the gates, and I walk through into the pleasant and inviting courtyard. It is exceptionally green today with birds singing and playfully fluttering from tree to tree. I grab a piece of fruit from one—it's like the juiciest, sweetest plum you could ever imagine.

A blue bird flies right up to me and stays eye level before me. His dark eyes seem to have a clear, glossy covering on them as he stares into mine. Reaching out slowly, I run my hand from his head down his soft back. He sings a little tune then flies away to the others in the trees.

A soothing female voice takes me by surprise saying, "Come, come into the glory of the Lord Most High." I am looking around but see no one, only Aedhel and Durward on the other side of the closed gates. I walk down the center path between the grass and trees of this living courtyard. A swooshing sound catches my attention, and I notice a movement to my right. Tall, white spirea shrubs expand from the courtyard wall, and I am pretty sure that I saw them moving. "Come, come into the glory of the Lord Most High," says the soothing voice again. The bounteous flowers of the spirea shrub begin to move and form into large faces of women. I am wondering why I have never noticed these shrubs before. Maybe it is because I am usually too busy talking when I come with the others on Day One. I am not sure, but every little thing seems to catch my eye today and appear as new.

Before me are bushes of red roses lining the walls on both sides of the arched opening which leads to the town square of the City of Angels. I enter to a commotion of angels moving about seemingly busy and talking with one another. I don't see Yeshua yet so I step off to the side to wait. The golden cobblestone road feels smooth under my feet. I run my big toe along the groove around one of the golden rectangles. Gold is such a common commodity here, yet on earth people will spend their whole life trying to attain it. It's here in abundance, along with every precious stone and metal.

The double doors of the Holy Library suddenly fly open with a loud noise, and I recognize Grandma's teacher, Raimo, as he steps out onto the steps. "Here they come!" he shouts in a loud voice. The angels line up in front of the library and along the side of the road which leads to Elohim's throne, and I realize that I am now standing alone. The sounds of marching and chanting come into recognition, and what looks like an army of angels become visible through the bright light on the golden path. Leading the army on his white horse, sits Yeshua—looking tall and strong. The angels each carry a sword and are dressed in tight fitting armored clothing. The scene is breathtaking. I take a mental image of this so I can show Jense tonight. *He'll freak.*

Yeshua sees me standing here, mouth open and all. He lifts his hand in a fist and the army stops. Turning Oleksander to face them, he says something to the leading angel, then moves to the side out of their way. The lead angel shouts, "March on!" They begin their marching again.

Yeshua smiles at me and rides my way, wearing his casual riding clothes. He reaches down his hand to me, and as his sleeve inches up I notice the scar at his wrist—the place where he was once nailed to a post in crucifixion. I have wondered why he still carries his scars—he could've taken them away. Yet each time I see them, I am reminded of his sacrifice and deep love for mankind . . . *for me.*

"Come on," he tells me and pulls me up. I hold on tight as we ride Oleksander up the golden street toward the circular castle, where the throne room of God is hidden inside. The closer we get the stronger the smell. It is a warm, woodsy scent—God's scent.

Yeshua helps me down and takes my hand, leading me into his majestic home past the angels who are standing alert and tall. I feel extremely small walking into such a vast space where fifteen foot cherubim can easily move about. The floors are marbled with gold, and columns made of different jewels—sapphire, emerald, and ruby to name a few —line the wide hallway that leads to a tall arch of double doors. They begin to open, bright light bursting through. Yeshua unexpectedly grabs my hand and pulls me aside.

"In here," he says, leading me to a small room off to the left. He shuts me alone inside, and I stand in sort of a stupor wondering what that was all about. There is a little bit of a distant commotion and then deafening silence. In the midst of the silence comes a strange feeling in my stomach. This is something I haven't felt since my days as a mortal. It takes me back to a little shop in New Orleans. There was something in that place that couldn't be explained in the natural, something dark. Someone is approaching, and I am almost sure that the door is going to open.

"All hail the king," says a sort of raspy voice right outside the door.

The voice did not feel right, and his tone had a hint of rebellious sarcasm in it—something I haven't heard as an immortal. I run over to the window to see if I can catch a glimpse. Three creatures stand equal in height. Two are definitely cherubim, and the third resembles a cherub, but something is different about him. The two seem to be escorting the one away from the castle. They let go of his arms, and he turns so that I see his face. He looks like a man, paler than me, with crystal eyes that are almost absent in color and a bald head. He flaps his two upper wings and then stretches all four of them out and open wide. His wings are white like the others but different—paler—as if they've been drained of their color, and the eyes on his wings are closed. There is something on his back that the other cherubim do not have—it looks like two pipes built into his skin, sticking up just above his wings. I notice strange scars all over his body. They are not noticeable upon first glance until you really stare. The two other cherubim stand tall and still, wings relaxed at their sides. They make no movement as the defiant one flaps his wings all at once and lets out a contemptuous laugh. His color begins to slowly darken until his skin is the color of ash, and his wings and eyes turn as black as coal.

"What do you think of your accuser?"

I jump. I was so caught up in that unsettling creature that I hadn't realized Yeshua had come back into the room.

Befuddled, I try to answer intelligently but there is nothing, "I'm not sure, Lord." I look out the window again, and the three are gone.

"They will escort him back. He cannot come on his own, nor can he enter the Garden, ever."

"He can change his appearance," I say, still searching out the window.

"Come sit down, Coco."

I take a seat next to him on the velvet couch and realize that I am just now putting the garment down for the first time since my traveling.

"He was made to reflect light, but now he is only an imitator. He has chosen darkness. He was beautiful—you would've been amazed. Jewels were embedded in his body, covering him with colors that sparkled against his bright light. And the music that came from his very being . . . it is indescribable, too glorious for words."

"So that explains the scars and the pipes. Can he still play?"

"No, he has been stripped of his glory."

I am silent, but my mind is buzzing.

"Coco, answers will come in time. But I will tell you this —deception is deceptive, and glory can be blinding."

I think about his words. "I was blind once, but here I am because of you."

"You are right that I paid a price for you, but you made the choice to believe and to follow me."

"I'm so glad I did. Thank you."

His smile is affectionate. "Thank *you*, Coco."

Wow. Did he really just thank me? There is no greater honor for me than to hear my king say those words. Everything in me wants to throw myself at his feet as I am suddenly aware of how blessed I am. I could've missed this—heaven, life with him and my family. I could have made other choices . . . so many times throughout my life I did. It wasn't until we moved to California that I even began really knowing about Yeshua. The boarding school I was in wasn't spiritually based. It was all about academics and etiquette and making a place for yourself in the world. I was taught to look nice and act nice, all for the motive of being better than others and to make a name for myself. I was on the road to worldly success, but as perfect as I seemed to be, I felt empty.

My mom and I started going to church with Aunt Claire's family, and I definitely had my walls up. First of all, I was still trying to warm up to my mother. I hadn't lived with her for most of my life, and as I've said before, there were long periods of time when I didn't hear from her. I wasn't sure how to respond to this new side of her that wanted to suddenly be with me. And the whole God thing was not something I was sure about either. But I was hungry for love, and I heard it through that speaker at the church. He somehow had the right words that I needed to hear, and it didn't take long before I was drawn in and wanting to know this God that he spoke of week after week. I didn't make a big show about it though. I knew everyone was wanting me to go down for prayer, and I was too prideful to give them that pleasure. Instead, I prayed in my room alone. I asked for forgiveness, and I made a commitment to follow him and live for him. There weren't many tears initially. I hadn't committed many sins, or so I thought. Then, as the months went by sitting in teaching after teaching, I suddenly began seeing all of the "stuff." No, I hadn't done many big outward acts of sin, but inwardly I was sinning all of the time. I soon realized how badly I needed a savior. That is when my life began to really change. I had a peace that I hadn't known my whole life. I suddenly cared about people and wanted to see others succeed. I wanted to sing songs to God and worship him—it wasn't scary anymore. My mother got to see some of that change before the accident. For that I am now so grateful because I know she is able to have peace about me.

A tear streams down my face. It is a tear of thankfulness.

Yeshua knows what I am thinking and feeling.

"You made your mother proud, and you have made me proud." He wipes the tear away then holds my face in his hands. "I know you are thankful, but I would like to see you smile, *and* I would like to see what you have made for me."

I nod and laugh and take a moment to wipe my face and gather myself. I stand, and removing the protective bag that Grandma made, I hold the garment up in front of me.

"Yes," he says, looking it over. "Would you put it on me?"

"Of course."

He stands looking into the large mirror hanging on the wall, and I cloak the winged robe around him, then step back to see how he looks. *Woah. Did I really make this?*

"It is perfect. Perfect, perfect, perfect," he says, grabbing my arms and giving me a shake. My dress begins to turn a bright yellow, and I am literally glowing. I look down and we both laugh.

"Thank you, Coco. Let's show Father. . . . Come," he says, walking out of the door. I have to walk fast to catch up to him, and I follow him down the large hallway to the doors that lead to the throne of God. A corner table holds a beautiful arrangement of flowering plants and a bowl of fruit. Yeshua grabs one of the fruit for me.

"Eat," he tells me.

I take the fruit with shaking hands. This is the throne room of God. The only other time that I've been here was the day that I entered the Garden. I am not afraid, but—ha! —nervous?—yeah, I think I might be.

The doors open and it is bright, but my eyes quickly adjust. Stepping onto the glass floor from the marble doesn't feel much different, both are smooth and cool. But looking down, it's as if I could fall right through. It is crystal—a large expanse of glass with no end to the sea of stars below, and to get to the throne you must walk across it.

We walk, Yeshua and I together, and for a quick second I am reminded of the story of Peter walking on the water with our Lord.

There seems to be no ceiling, just an open sky of white. I see Elohim ahead sitting on his throne. Two cherubim are off to each side, and flying right above him are the strangest creatures I have ever seen. They are the same size as the cherubim, but they are red in color and have six wings. The set of two wings in the middle are keeping them afloat, while the other sets are covering their face and their feet. They fade from view so that I no longer see them. *Seraphim.* I have heard of them, but this is my first time to see them. Elohim is talking to twenty-four beings who are sitting on stationary thrones in two rows of twelve off to the side. They have the appearance of men and women of old age—wrinkles and white hair—but they somehow still look youthful and vibrant. They are each wearing a crown. Just like the seraphim, I have never seen the twenty-four elders before, but I have heard of them.

"Son, daughter!" roars Elohim, pausing his conversation and welcoming us to come closer. "Coco, the elders and I were just talking about Sena, and your grandmother was in our conversation too. They are bringing us the robes for our Great Feast."

"And Coco has made mine, Father." Yeshua stretches his arms down and out, showing off the garment that I made for him. I am still amazed.

"Ah, yes. Faithful Coco! It is just as perfect before my very eyes. Very fitting for you, son."

Elohim's feet rest on the glass floor, and it is hard to distinguish between the two. I suddenly realize that the elders are gone, disappearing like the seraphim I presume. Although I can not see them, I am certain that they are still here in their same spots. The cherubim take a place next to the throne, and using their wings to cover themselves they disappear from my sight just as the others have. It is now only Elohim, Yeshua, and myself—well, visible anyway.

"Coco, I want to give you a gift. What would you like, my darling?"

I take a moment to think, not wanting to answer hastily.

"Father, I have all that I could need or want here. I could only ask that you keep my mom and my dad safe, and that I may see them here someday."

"Yes, I have shown you your father, and your mother is well too."

A cherub comes back into view, and he walks over to a table with a large bowl on top.

"Come here, I want to show you something," he says, motioning with his hand for me to come closer.

I approach his throne, and he gently pulls me next to him and turns me so that I am facing in the same direction that he is. His touch felt cool and smooth, like the glass under my feet. The cherub places the table in front of me, and I now see that the large bowl is full of water.

"Look," says Elohim.

I stare into the water, and an image of my mother comes into view. There is a man kneeling in front of her, and I am understanding that it is a marriage proposal. I am surprised and cover my mouth. She looks so happy. My mother has never been married. She didn't know who my father was, and she had plenty of men in her life as I was younger, but in the last couple of years of my mortal life there was no one.

"Does he know you, Lord?"

"Yes, Coco. Mark is a noble man. She is in good hands." He takes his finger and stirs the water. I see them again, but this time they are sitting together on a couch, and mom is holding a baby in her arms. "You will meet her. Her name is Beverly."

"A sister?" It is a question and a statement. "Thank you,

Lord. Thank you so much."

I turn and give him a hug and a kiss, and he laughs and kisses me back.

"Father, I request that Coco stay at the palace tonight—if she'd like. I have a special meal planned to thank her."

"Yes, tomorrow is your Day One, Coco. You can return then with the others."

"I would love to!"

"Then I will send word to your family," says Elohim.

Yeshua grabs my hand to walk me out, but I stop and turn to face Elohim again.

"One more thing, Lord?"

"Yes, dear?"

"Jense would love to see his mother and father. Will there be an Opening soon for them?"

"There will be one right now. Leone."

The cherub gives a nod and then fades his appearance until he is gone.

"Thank you, Lord."

Walking next to Yeshua on that sea of glass, all I can think about is the look on my mom's face while holding her new child—my sister. Knowing her deep pain of losing me—her only daughter—in a tragic car accident, I only have feelings of joy for her and our new family.

I follow Yeshua down the hall to a different room than before. It is smaller and dimmer than the other rooms with only lamps for its light. White shutters are sealed closed, blocking any light that would try to enter through the only window on one of the tall, navy blue walls. Furniture is sparse—a writing desk, a bookshelf, and an oversized chair with an ottoman—but any more and it would not fit.

"I hope this room suits you. I know how much you like to read, and there are plenty of books in here to intrigue you."

"Are you going somewhere?" I ask.

"I do have some business to attend to tonight, but I have a special breakfast planned for us in the morning. Angels are available for anything that you may need in the meantime."

I nod my head, "Thank you."

He puts his hands straight out together and gives a quick bow. "Good night."

Watching him leave is never fun, but I try to think of what breakfast will be like in the morning. Like a light board, my thoughts quickly switch to wondering what kind of business he is tending to tonight. Knowing that I could not know the answer, I resign to picking out a book that might keep my attention long enough.

THE HIDDEN TREASURE OF SKYLARK titles one of the books. *Hmmm, what is this one about?*

I melt into the cushy chair and wrap the chocolate colored fleece blanket around me. A glass pitcher of orange juice sits upon the side table along with a small glass. Actually, orange juice sounds perfect right now. And it is perfect—sweet with a slight hint of tartness and lots of pulp, just the way that I like it. I open the book and begin to read, but my eyes are feeling heavy, and I realize how tired I suddenly am.

I'll close them just for a moment.

Resting the book on my chest, I fall quickly into a deep sleep. My mind is a blank slate—no dreams, thoughts, or memories—just a time for my spirit to recuperate from such an eventful day. It is a peaceful darkness. So peaceful that I am confused to find myself with eyes open now and staring up at the ceiling.

I close my eyes again and slowly fall back into unconsciousness when . . . loud sounds pull me out of my slumber. In my state of half-sleep I am pretty sure that I hear rain—pouring rain—and . . . *thunder?*

9. SECRETS REVEALED

I glance around the room trying to make sense of what I am hearing. Is it raining? I set the book on the ottoman and curiously hurry to the window to take a peek. Unlatching the tall shutters, they slowly open on their hinge, and it is clear that it is not raining—at least not outside.

Again, peals of thunder.

Puzzled and curious, I rush to the door, and because I am unsure of what I will find, I turn the knob slowly and open it just enough to see into the hallway. It is empty and all is quiet. I know what I heard, but I see no evidence of any occurrence, only two angels gradually appearing at the outside of the throne room doors. *Did they appear because of me?*

The sound of music—harps maybe—plays from inside, grasping my attention, and I decide to inquire of one of the angels. I slowly approach, glancing into each opened room as I pass, hoping I will see Yeshua in one of them, but I see no one.

The playing gets louder the closer I get, and the angels get taller.

"What is going on inside?" I ask the one on the right, but neither of them answer me.

"May I go in and see?" Again, no answer. I reach for the golden handle.

"Stop," orders the angel.

I jump and withdraw my hand.

"Here," he says, beckoning me with his finger. Running it along the door, he makes the shape of a rectangle, creating some sort of opening so that I may see inside. I look up at the angel, and he nods.

What is this? Thousands of men and women are standing before Elohim and Yeshua, and everyone is dressed in white —the same type of clothing we all enter the Garden in. I can't tell where the music is coming from, but harps are playing, and everyone begins to sing a song that I have never heard before.

"Who are they?" I ask, but still I get no answer. I am realizing that these angels are not like the teachers that I am used to being around. It is not clear whether they lack the answers or if they are just not allowed to tell me. I don't press any further.

Inside, three angels fly above the people. I can't quite make out what they are saying, but I do hear bits and pieces of something about judgement. I am startled by the touch of the angels hand on my ear. Warmth works its way down my ear canal, and my hearing opens up so that the music inside is loudly playing. The third angel shouts out, and I can hear him clearly now as if there is no barrier between us. "If anyone worships the beast and his image, and receives his mark on his forehead or on his hand, he himself shall also drink of the wine of the wrath of God."

My stomach drops, not in fear but in deep sorrow. The end really is coming. Just as strong and real as the sorrow that I feel, now excitement begins to rise and take over. *My family. They will be here soon.*

The images through the angelic window become hazy and now a blur as the opening dissolves into the door so that it is no more. I look up at the angel standing tall and staring straight ahead.

"Thank you," I say to the statuesque creature, but of course, no reply.

Walking back to my room, the same questions flood my mind that I've been wondering since my visit with Amraphel. We all know that Yeshua is returning to the earth to gather his people before the Great Judgement begins. But when? It must be soon. And what about the man who is the antichrist? Are my mother or father affected by his rule? Do they know who he is? Question after question. Instantly, I am reminded of what Elohim showed me. My mother and her family were so happy. Elohim assured me that I would see them and my father, and I believe him, but still I wonder how everything will play out.

"Pst." The noise comes from behind me, interrupting my thoughts. I turn and see Yeshua, and I am so excited that I run and hug him.

He laughs. "Are you ready for breakfast?"

Did I really sleep that long? I *am* hungry, not just for food but for answers. "Yes, that would be great," I reply with relief, knowing that Yeshua will satisfy my intrigue.

To my surprise we walk right out the front doors of the palace where Oleksander waits.

"I was thinking a picnic would be nice."

"Fun! I love picnics."

He takes my hand to help me onto the horse. We ride down the main road which leads back to the town square, but then leave the path and ride out into an open meadow of wild flowers of every kind. Up ahead I can see a square, wooden table with a lacy tablecloth draped over top. Crystal plates and glasses for two await, separated by a short vase of some of the picked flowers.

"It's beautiful," I tell him as he helps me to my feet.

Yeshua pulls one of the chairs back for me to sit, and an angel appears holding a silver carafe.

"What would you like to drink?" he asks me.

"Apple juice, please."

"My king?" he gives Yeshua a bow.

"I would like orange juice. Thank you, Ahmiel."

The angel pours my juice first, then out of the same carafe he fills Yeshua's glass with orange juice. He fades from sight as food appears on our plates. Two slices of brioche french toast are neatly placed against each other with hazelnuts sprinkled over top. A bowl of berry compote sits next to a small glass pitcher of maple syrup.

We both eat and enjoy the mixture of flavors. Everything is so delicious. Now that my strength is regained, I'm wanting to ask him about all of the things that are churning inside.

"I understand that you have questions for me," Yeshua interjects, breaking the silence.

"Yes, I have many actually," I admit.

"Well, let's hear some."

"*Okay*. Well, I saw the people—"

"Yes," he intercepts, reminding me that I don't need to explain because he already knows.

"Will the Gathering happen soon?" I finally blurt out. I wasn't sure if he'd actually answer me or if I would get something vague, but he nods.

"Yes, it must happen soon. Prophecy is being fulfilled."

"I mean, like soon, soon?"

"Yes," he smiles, "very soon, soon."

"What is it like on the earth right now? I mean, Amraphel showed me the antichrist so it must be pretty bad."

He is not surprised by any of my questions, nor is he bothered by the fact that I show concern for my family. But it's not just my family—it's the many other lives on the earth today that I feel for as well.

"Coco, these things must happen." He pauses, and then he smiles. "I can tell you that your family is not directly being affected. And those who are, well you saw many of them today. They will receive their reward. Believe me, it is not in vain."

I am relieved that my family is not suffering, and remembering the people before the throne puts everything into perspective. They were so happy, and now they are safe —the hardships are over. The things that they went through will only be a faded memory now. No one can take this away from them—no man and not even Satan himself. I soon place those thoughts aside as I see what looks like pain in the eyes of my Lord.

Pain. It's not something I feel often here, but right now, I feel it. My chest closes tightly, and the feeling of deepest heartache encompasses so much that I cannot take it. I feel like I could die, yet I am already dead. How is this so? The agony. The loss. The unfulfilled destinies. I buckle over in my seat, and just when I think that my chest will surely burst open, it lets go and is lifted from me. I sit, still bent over, with my eyes closed as peace strengthens me to my previous state.

"It will end. It must," he whispers.

I slowly lift myself upright and nod. I have felt a taste of the Father's pain. The type of pain that I imagine only a parent could feel. I have never had a child of my own—

never known the feeling a parent has when their child rebels or separates from their family.

Aunt Claire led a prayer group in her home, and occasionally my mother would go. I remember going with her once, and I will never forget the tired face of one of the women in that group. The other women were smiling and laughing, talking about things like the purse they just bought and the movie that they saw over the weekend. One lady complained about wanting to replace her carpet, but that woman just sat there silent through all of the small talk. She was friendly, and she would even give a polite smile during the conversation, but it wasn't until the prayer requests were offered that I understood the puffy eyes and the lines that marked her forehead. Aunt Claire reminded the group of Debbie's son who was addicted to a certain drug. Debbie lowered her face into her hands. Aunt Claire explained that she hadn't heard from him in weeks and she wasn't sure where he was staying, or if he was okay.

I imagine that the pain of that mother longing for her son to come home and be set free is only a fraction of what I just felt.

"I want to show you something." His voice is kind and gentle.

I don't know if I can take any more, but he assures me, "You will like it."

I take his offered hand, and as we walk, the tall flowers hit against our legs, and a warm breeze blows my loosened pieces of hair against my face. The questions are gone. My uneasiness has subsided. Perfect peace washes through me. Walking up to the edge of the cliff that we are on, all I can see are thick clouds rising up toward us.

"Watch," he says, pointing. The clouds continue to ascend quickly, and as they reach us our hair and clothing are blown straight back. I shut my eyes from the cool force, letting it hit my face, and then—just like that—it is gone. As

I open them, I can see green throughout the Garden below in all of its expanse. It is breathtakingly beautiful. I wonder if I can see anyone from this far. I do have telephoto vision when needed, but we are up very high. I focus on a spot and zoom my sight, but I can't make anything out. Yeshua's hand touches my back, and suddenly I have clear vision of people, stirring like ants below—many, many people. In fact, it looks as though every community is gathering and waiting at their own set of gates. Taking my sight back in, I look at Yeshua with a quizzical face.

"Everyone is coming today. It was announced while you were away. The gates will be closed, so we will all meet along the base of the mountain."

"Why are the gates closed to us, Lord?"

"Father will explain everything, Coco. Things are changing, but remember—it's a good change."

He smiles to reassure me and it works. My excitement returns.

"Take a moment for yourself . . . I will be right over there waiting for you." He points toward the table where an angel is standing with a document of some sort in his hand. Yeshua transports to him, and they join in an immediate discussion.

Take a moment for yourself. Sighing, I relax my spirit body and breathe in the fresh air. This will be the first time that all seven communities will be gathered at the same time since my being here. I wonder what everyone is thinking about today's gathering. Again, using my telephoto sight I try to see the assemblage of people below. I cannot see them, so for fun I survey the land, catching sight of magnified birds as my eyes pass across. Every community is flourishing with life, reminding me of how blessed I truly am. I close my eyes breathing in another deep breath. *Thank you, Father.*

✦

Yeshua and I ride into the city square and into the courtyard where he lets me off at the gates.

"Thank you for your delightful presence, Coco."

It doesn't feel adequate, but I have no other way of expressing my gratitude in this moment, so I simply say, "Thank you, Yeshua."

Aedhel opens the gates for me, and I spot my family waiting on the other side.

Jense pulls me into his arms and gives me a big bear hug. Gramps kisses the top of my head, and Grandma kisses my cheek. They are all smiles and elation.

"Wow, I feel missed."

"Maybe a little," says Jense with a jesting grin. He and Grandma take my hand, and together we transport to stand next to the rest of our family.

"I have so much to show you," I whisper to Jense.

"From the throne room?" he asks.

"Oh, . . . well . . . that's not what I was thinking."

"What then? Show me."

"You're like a little boy when you get excited. It's amusing."

"Show me," he says, grabbing my arm and fitting my hand in his.

Laughing, I pull my hand back. "I will show you later, Jense."

A trumpet sounds from the sky above us, getting everyone's attention and bringing all of the chatter and whispers to a silence. We all know that something different is happening today, but we are not quite sure what it is, although I have my suspicions. All eyes are now on the angel who stands above us on a cloud. An image of Elohim and Yeshua sitting on thrones is projected into the sky next to the angel. I was just with Yeshua in riding clothes, but now he wears a white robe—not the one I made for him, but a simpler one, brightly glowing on his radiant body. He also wears a golden crown on his head.

He stands from his throne, and without thinking everyone bows their knee in reverence. His presence is that commanding, that compelling.

"Rise," affirms Elohim.

We all stand—still weak in our knees—and music begins to play. Everything seems as usual. We sing and dance together, and worship our God. We rejoice at those who have been added to the kingdom as we see their faces pass, just as the weeks before. But today there is an energy unlike any other. Today there is an expectation for something great.

Yeshua stands, beaming. And looking out across the valley at all of the people, I realize . . . so are we. Our conjoined light is so bright, it's as if we are all one—one bright, glorious light. Elohim himself lets out a high-powered laugh, and everyone begins to cheer.

As the commotion dies down and we regain our composure, the angel on the cloud lifts his hands as if waiting to make an important announcement.

Giving our full attention, Elohim's voice speaks out, "The Time Has Come." The ground shakes.

Though everyone remains silent, there is no mistaking that the impact of his words are felt by all. We wait for further explanation, and with anticipation I feel a surging in my chest.

The angel lowers his hands and a white cloud from above descends and hovers in front of Yeshua.

The angel proclaims, "The time has come for you to gather your harvest."

Yeshua steps out onto the cloud with a look of readiness on his face. Three angels come into view and take their place around him.

Everyone knows what this means, but no one can say a word. It is like we are all dumbfounded, astonished that this is really finally happening.

"Go, son," whispers Elohim.

Yeshua gives us a kind smile and then, along with the three angels, fades out of sight.

Elohim speaks up in a fatherly tone, "Children, change is here. We will not meet together again until the Great Feast. The gates will remain closed, and no one can enter Alpha until my judgment has been completed on the earth. Go and prepare homes for your families. Rejoice, for you will reunite soon, and then we will share together in what we have been preparing for! Rejoice, children!"

With that the sky is back to before with no sight of him or the angel. Just as he said, the gates remain closed and will until the time of the Great Feast.

10. FIRST IMPRESSIONS

Still reeling from the buzz of today's announcement, Jense and I stumble into the doorway of the plantation house; Gramps and Grandma follow in behind us.

"Can you believe this," Jense says for probably the fifth time.

"My darlings will really be here," sings Grandma, clasping her hands together.

I remember my sister—the one they know nothing about yet.

"Beverly," I blurt out.

"Who's that, sugar?" asks Grandma.

"My sister . . . your granddaughter," I stammer.

"What?" Grandma inquires.

"Elohim showed her to me. Mom is married to Mark and they have a baby—her name is Beverly."

It looks as though a light bulb goes off in Grandma's head.

"We missed the Opening," she admits. "Elohim wanted all of the robes brought in, so Gramps and some of the other men helped us take them to the gates. We heard the chimes, but we didn't make it in time."

I don't like seeing Grandma disappointed, so I put my hand on her arm and try to make her feel better.

"You will see them soon for yourself, Grandma. You will touch them with your own hands and hold them in your arms."

Her smile returns, and a tear falls from the outer edge of her eye.

"Yes." She breathes in and relaxes her shoulders.

"What's this?" Gramps calls, standing at the dining table.

We gather around him to see two sets of building plans. One for a two-story cottage with the names Mark and Nicole written across the top, and the other, of course, is Brody and Claire's beach bungalow.

"Looks like we have some houses to build," he concedes.

"I don't understand . . . how long do we have left in the Garden? Is it really worth building houses if we will leave soon?" I ask.

"Well, Coco, these building plans are from the throne, and if Elohim says we should build houses then there must still be enough time to use them."

"How long do you think we have before they get here?" asks Grandma.

"Oh, I don't know. . . . I suppose it will take days for everyone to see Elohim and enter the Garden . . . maybe weeks. He rubs the side of his face contemplating the situation.

"Unless they all see Elohim together, at once," I submit. "I saw this . . . at the palace. There was a large gathering . . . thousands of people. They had to have entered together or at least within the same time frame."

They stare at me taking in the knowledge.

"Yes, that is an option," says Gramps. "Well, if we don't finish in time, our house is open. And Mark and Brody would like time reuniting with their families I'm sure." He studies the blueprints some more. "I think we can get this knocked out pretty quick though."

Obviously we have Jense's family and mine to build for, but there's also cousins and other family members coming in too.

"I'm sure everyone's starting to gather now, so I better go join them and work out a plan," explains Gramps, collecting his things.

By "everyone" he means all of our family on the plantation—years and years worth of people. Thankfully we have a large line of family available to help each immediate family with their building needs.

"What should Jense and I do, Grandma?"

"Well, I think you kids should continue with the tending and trading for now. I'll get you to help me with decorating when the time comes. You'll probably want to do your own room."

My room? Her words take me by surprise. I hadn't thought of that. Partly I am excited, but mostly I feel sort of sad—okay, really sad. Being with Gramps and Grandma . . . and Jense—and what about Jense? The building plans were for a beach bungalow. That means Jense will be moving to the coast. I know it's only fifteen miles away, but I will miss seeing Jense everyday and sharing evenings with the four of us playing games. It's not that I don't miss my mother or that she has been replaced. It's just that we've formed a special bond, the four of us, and lived out so many happy memories in this house together.

In my heart I hear Yeshua's voice, "It's a good change." I remind myself a couple more times. *It's a good change. It's a good change.* I am feeling better now.

Grandma seems to know what Jense and I both are thinking.

"We've had some good times here together, haven't we?"

She pulls both of us into a group hug.

"We'll still be close. Coco, you'll be here on the plantation . . . and we all know that the coast is one of our favorite places to be—just a snap of the fingers and I'm there."

She snaps her fingers to make a point, and we all smile and shake off the sadness.

"Yes, I will treasure our memories . . . good, good memories."

Jense holds up his hand and lifts his brows as if remembering something important.

"Speaking of treasures, Coco and I have something for you."

I decide that saying the words "We do?" aloud is not the best, so I think it instead.

Jense returns holding a rectangular, white-washed wooden box with a carved floral pattern on the top and along the sides. He gives me the look like I know what's inside so I keep quiet, trying to remember. The past two days have been so eventful that it's all I've been thinking about.

"Well, what's this?" she gasps.

Jense is beaming. "Open it up and see."

The box opens and immediately the smoothness of the glossy pink pearls resting on the waves of white silk causes my heart to melt, and by the sound of it, Grandma's too.

"Oh my," she says, eyes already teary.

"You finished it!" I exclaim and throw my arms around his neck.

"Jense, it's beautiful," she marvels.

"Well, you are beautiful, Grandma."

"Oh, you sweetheart, you. Come here." She gives him a big hug and I join in, wrapping my arms around the both of them.

"It's stunning. I haven't seen anything like this—thank you," she says taking Jense's face in her hands, and standing on her toes she kisses his cheek, then turns to kiss mine. "Thank you both."

She picks it up out of the box and motions to Jense, "Put it on me, would ya?"

"Yes ma'am." Jense's fingers fumble with the clasp until it's latched and then takes a step aside so that we can see.

Standing in front of the wall mirror, we all gape at the strand of gems resting on Grandma's chest. Her smooth hand caresses them and looking at our reflections she says, "A treasure from my treasures."

We put our arms around each other and hold on as if we are holding on to precious memories that could never be replaced. And as we let go of one another, its like we are surrendering to a new chapter—not forgetting the old, but welcoming new memories and new adventures.

I turn to walk away when suddenly I feel a strange tingle in my body starting with my feet and working it's way up. I turn back to see if anyone else is feeling this, and by their confused looks my guess is that they are.

"What's going on?" I ask Grandma.

"I'm not sure. Do you feel it too, Jense?"

"Yes ma'am," he says, patting at his chest.

The door flies open, and like a gush of wind moving through the house, it's as if I'm in a fairy tale where the spell is broken and everything cursed suddenly becomes new. The force moves through me, and looking down I see skin— real skin . . . and real fingernails. My dress is no longer an image, it is fabric made of fibers and thread. I lift a piece up and away from my body to get a closer look, and I notice the scar that was on my left hand as a mortal has not returned. Jense grabs me and we look into each other's face. He pulls at my cheeks and laughs.

"It's the old you, Coco, but even better!"

"You too!" I say excitedly.

We both look and see Grandma who is examining herself in the mirror. Immediately, we are standing next to her.

"Well, we can still transport—"

"Can you believe this," she interrupts me. She is running her finger across the fine wrinkles under her eyes. "It's me," she says. She looks the same really, only a few small wrinkles and a freckle on her forehead—a birthmark maybe —that wasn't there before. She still looks young and vibrant only now in a glorified body.

A thought suddenly hits me. "What about Lion and Letty?" I ask aloud.

They follow me as I run out the open door.

"I'm going to find Gramps," Grandma calls.

"Okay!" we yell back.

I can't explain how the Garden is different, but it is. It doesn't make sense because it seemed real before, but now . . . it really is real. I feel the same. No tire from running, and I'm not short of breath. The same, just in my old body—but it isn't old, it's new. Jense jumps over me just to see if he still can. He touches ground in a stumble and I laugh at his awkward landing.

"Just need a little practice," he says.

The door at Christy's house is wide open. Jense races me inside where we see Lion and Letty playing on the floor in real bodies—bodies that look like a five year old would have. Christy walks into the room.

"He advanced their mortal bodies too," I state and question all at once.

"Yes," she says, still amazed. "What does all of this

mean?"

"It means the Gathering happened, doesn't it?" I ask, looking at Jense.

"That would be my guess."

"Then we better go and see how we can help with the houses," Christy asserts.

"You're right," I reply.

Jense rubs his hands together. "Kids, let's go try out these new bodies—we have work to do."

✦

When I read *cottage*, I pictured something from a Thomas Kincade painting. And when I read *beach bungalow*, I pictured the house that is standing before me now. But they tell me that this one is the cottage. What do I know about house types?—I was raised on a campus where I slept in a dormitory. I do know that I like the light green exterior with the cream colored trim and shutters. And I like the dark rocking chairs on the front porch.

It's unbelievable to think that this place was built in four days. Even the landscaping is almost finished, thanks to Aunt Tildie who's been planting away all morning.

Grandma steps out onto the porch in a white collared blouse and slacks. Her perfume reaches out to grab me. I love the narcissus mixed with fruit—a warm and spicy scent that I've come to recognize as my grandmother's fragrance.

"Oh, there you are, Coco. Are you ready to see your new house?"

"I am," I chirp.

Stepping inside to the black and white tiled entryway is like having a tall glass of sweet tea in Grandma's kitchen—instant comfort. Anyone who knows my mother has heard her say at some time or another how much she likes black and white tile. The rest of the house appears to have dark wood flooring, at least on the first level. I run my finger across the smooth, scalloped edge of the glass top table sitting empty against the cream colored wall. It's a perfect place for a family photograph and a fresh bouquet of flowers.

Grandma and my aunts have done an exquisite job at decorating—from rugs to window treatments, throw pillows and blankets. I helped Grandma shop some at the market, but I left the decorating to the experts. I decided that even my room was better in their hands.

We pass a large bedroom and I can't help but notice the two pillows resting on the white comforter. Yellow songbirds on a mint green and tiffany blue floral print. I smile remembering back to my mother's bird collection. My favorite was a large porcelain bird that sat on her kitchen counter—it was the prettiest sea green with cutouts along the side so that a candle's light could glow through. Walking past the kitchen now, I can't believe my eyes.

"Are you kidding me? I was just thinking of this bird!" An exact replica is sitting on top of the counter. "Where did you find this, Grandma?"

"At the market. I couldn't believe it at first. It was right out in front on Ruben's display. I knew it was for Nicole."

"She's gonna love it. That is so cool!"

"Yes, she's gonna love it," Grandma agreed. "Come on, let's go see your room."

The white stairs with their dark wooden tops remind me of piano keys leading up to a hallway between three bedrooms and a bathroom.

"You get the big room to the left. I think you're going to like it," she calls, still climbing the stairs.

The door opens to something out of the page of a magazine. *Wow.* This is more elaborate than my simple room at Gramps' and Grandma's. Peachy walls with cream-colored trim and two large built in bookcases set the mood for comfort. An eclectic, crystal chandelier hangs above the bed of large coral-colored flowers with hints of turquoise and large lime-green leaves. A writing desk holds a turquoise glass vase full of white peonies and a set of stationary with a large "C" in the top corner, held together with a coral-colored ribbon. Stepping onto the plush rug, my toes sink into its soft fur. I curl my toes to pull at its luxurious fibers.

"I'm in heaven." I expressively exhale.

Grandma laughs at my attempt at being funny. "Look in the closet, dear."

Closet? Right, I now wear clothes . . . and opening the door I see that I have plenty to choose from.

"Did you make these, Grandma?"

"No, I haven't had time to sew between this house and Claire's. There's a group of ladies that brought in clothes to the market." She is just starting to tell me something about blankets when the door knocks against the wall, stealing our attention. Jense is standing there, ghost-faced, taking on the definitive form of shock.

I'm trying to think of what awful thing could have happened to put him in such a state, but then a huge smile stretches across his face—light shimmers in his eyes.

"They're coming," he gushes.

Grandma and I both take in a loud breath, move around nervously, then cling onto one another's arm as we follow Jense down the stairs and out to the front yard.

Aunt Tildie is no where to be seen, but in the distance there are voices—excited voices—coming from every direction.

Exhilaration is a wild emotion that, in this moment, forces my spirit into an extreme state of euphoria. I feel as though I cannot contain it.

Staring out into the crowded herd of trees, I magnify my view but can't seem to make anything out clearly—only the fact that there is movement.

"Can you see them?" I ask, between chattering teeth.

"I can't tell," Grandma aspirates.

"There!" declares Jense.

I'm not sure the exact moment my feet left the ground. Was it when I saw my mother or the beautiful little girl walking beside her?

I run in utter desperation until I'm reminded of my ability to transport. It's a moment where everything seems to stand still as I break through the bounds of time and materialize before them.

We embrace, my mother and I. Her hands grab a hold of my hair, and I sink into her enveloping warmth, and we cry. Tears of healing first, then tears of joy.

She pulls my head back so that we can see each other's face.

"Hi," she says softly.

"Hi."

I take a step back to greet the tall man next to my mother and the little girl whom I already know about—thanks to Elohim.

"This is—"

"Mark," I say, cutting her off.

Mom smiles. "Yes. And—"

"Beverly," I once again interject.

The three of them laugh.

"*Okaay*," says mom, wrinkling her forehead.

"I take it you already know us?" Mark asks, extending his hand to me. I offer mine and he gently holds it between both of his.

"I know *of* you, but I am eager to get to know you both," I say, shifting my attention to my sister.

Retrieving my hand, I lower myself so that I am at eye level to the little brown-haired girl. Besides the chocolate hair and eyes, she looks a lot like me.

"Hi, Beverly," I say tenderly.

"Are you my sister?" she asks in her sweet voice.

"Yes," I affirm. "I'm Coco."

"I like your name."

"Thank you," I laugh.

We all seem to take in a deep breath as the realization sinks in that this is real—we really are together.

"Where is Aunt Claire?" I ask, searching behind me. I was certain that I saw her at the clearing along side of the others, but I don't see her now . . . or Jense—only Gramps and Grandma hugging and lightly rocking each other.

I transport to them, realizing that my family didn't join me but are walking instead.

"Sorry," I call out. "I will show you how. Or, maybe Gramps should—he taught me."

I turn to Gramps expecting a smile, but instead there are traces of tears on both his and Grandma's faces.

"What is it?" I ask. "Where's Jense and his family? I thought I saw Aunt Claire."

"Claire is here, Coco," Grandma says, settling me for a moment.

And then I realize . . . I saw Aunt Claire, but where was Uncle Brody? And Cheryl, Jense's sister, . . . where was she, and where was her husband, Reggie? *Didn't they come?* But Uncle Brody . . . he loved the Lord. Well, he went to church every Sunday. I am confused. Then I remember the Opening. Aunt Claire was crying because he left her. Did he leave the Lord too?

I barely get the words out, "Oh, no."

11. INVITATIONS

Aunt Claire returned a while ago, but Jense remained on the bank by the swimming hole. The same one we go to for the Opening.

"Give him some time, Coco," Grandma tells me.

I want to comfort him, but she is right, he needs time alone with the Lord.

I plop down on her porch swing. "You're right," I say. "I'll come inside soon, Grandma."

"Okay, darling," she says softly, shutting the screen door and walking away.

I hear the laughter from inside and wish Jense were here experiencing this sweet reunion.

"Lord, encourage Jense," I pray. A tangible peace settles over me reminding me that our perfect God is near. Yet, even in the midst of his peace there is a slight something unsettled inside of me. I search my heart until the answer comes—*my* dad.

Elohim told me he would be here so he must be somewhere in the Garden.

I realize that the unsettling is more of a nervous excitement. I just want to meet him and the rest of my family. Maybe tomorrow he will come. But I know he has other family members to reconnect with—his known ones. I determine that I should prepare my heart for waiting, just in case.

Blackbirds begin to sing and the lanterns switch on as clouds descend around the mountain of the Lord.

"Coco."

Jense's voice comes from behind me. It was calm and mellow, but I wasn't expecting it so I jump a little.

I turn to see a glow, the physical form of serenity in the shape of Jense's body. He has literally taken on the peace of God.

"Jense," I say softly.

He leaps onto the brick porch and takes a seat next to me. I'm not sure what to say or if I should hug him, so I just sit here staring at him.

"I saw my dad and my sister. Yeshua was with me and he created an Opening."

I lift my eyebrows and nod my head to show him that I understand, but still I remain silent.

"They believe now."

For a moment he joins me in silence and we lightly swing.

"The Millennium, that's when I'll see them," he starts again.

"Does your mom know?"

"Yeah, she knows."

I'm glad that Jense can hear them laughing inside the house. Gramps was right, Mark has gone to spend time with his parents, so it is only my grandparents with their daughters and Beverly. She has been entertaining them with stories and a wild imagination. Now, they are going through the photo book that Grandma got from the City of Angels, looking at old memories.

"Have you met your dad yet?" he asks me.

"No. That's what I was thinking about out here. Well, that and you of course."

He smiles and gives my leg a squeeze. I poke his side and we both laugh, then he puts his arm around my shoulder. I rest my head on his and we take in the moment—a moment we had dreamed of. The moment that is the ending and the beginning all at the same time. A moment where words are vacant, so we swing.

✦

Over a month has flown by and I have adjusted well to life in the cottage with my mom and our new family. Daily life is back to the way it was before, tending to the Garden and gathering for market. The only major difference is that we no longer go to Alpha on Day One. Instead we meet as a community in the open field. No angels or archangels, neither does Elohim or Yeshua come. Well, at least not in physical form, but there's no denying that their presence is there. We've spent evenings together, many nights at the plantation house, telling our newly arrived family members stories of what it was like to go to Alpha, to the City of Angels, and to the palace. They told us their stories of the Gathering and of the four days that they spent before coming to reunite with us. Mom said that because there were so many people they entered in groups of one hundred and fifty thousand, one group at a time, and instead of entering the gates, an angel would transport them in to the grassy land that leads to the palace. Our family members waited two days before going in, on some sort of an island apart from the Garden, where they were "pampered and treated like royalty" were her words.

Jense and I still spend most of our days together and take beach trips as before, and when we take the kids with us, Beverly comes too. She has made many friends and fits right in with Lion and Letty. Lansing continues to make his way to the plantation house every morning, I guess out of habit, but he always comes back to spend the nights with me. From my bedroom window I watch him jump up the steps and lay across the front porch behind where Gramps and Jense are sitting.

I start to pull away from the window when something catches my eye drawing me back in to see. A golden retriever is running down the path between our houses and heading straight for Jense who only just now becomes aware.

"Chipper?" He stands questioning.

Just like a movie scene, the dog runs right up to Jense and jumps up on him, licking him wherever he can. "Chip! It really is you!"

I materialize outside next to Jense and the friendly dog who now comes to greet me.

"What took you so long to get here?" I say as I take his ears and give a good rub.

Jense picks up a stick and throws it for the dog, initiating a game of retrieve. As the two run off to play, I take a seat next to Gramps.

"Looks like you have a visitor as well," he says, nodding his head towards the woods.

"Me?" I ask, expecting another animal, but instead I see a familiar looking man walking our way. I am still trying to get used to feeling an actual heart beating inside of me again. Right now it seems to be skipping beats.

"Is it my dad? I question Gramps.

"I do believe it is," he says and stands to welcome the stranger.

The man doesn't transport—he walks, looking at the houses and land as he passes them. My stomach turns and my skipping heart now picks up speed.

"Hello." He gives a short wave and comes to stand before us. "My name is Marten," he says with an accent I recognize as Swedish.

"Hi, Marten. I'm John and this is my granddaughter Coco."

He looks at me and smiles, searching my face, I suspect, for some sort of resemblance. I smile back, assuring him that he is welcome here.

"Yes," he says tenderly. "I would have come sooner only I just recently found out about you and I didn't know how to find you. I live in Zeta."

"And how did you find us today?" asks Gramps, purely out of curiosity.

"An angel. And the dog," he laughs. "They led me to you."

Now that he's here I'm not sure what to do, or what to say. I just stare at him. I, too, search his face for resemblance. I can see why my mother would have been drawn to him. He is average in size but very good looking, and he has a charming personality.

"Do you know who I am, Coco?"

"Yes, I have seen you and I have heard of you."

"From your mother?" he asks.

"No. Elohim. Mother did not know who my father was."

"I understand," he says. "And your mother, is she here?"

"I'll get her," says Gramps, then disappears.

"I have prayed for you," I say, breaking the moment of silence.

"Thank You." He emphasizes the words with a look of sincerity on his face. "I wish I would have known sooner. I would have come to you, on Earth. I would have been in your life. You could have stayed with me, in Sweden, during the summers, with my wife and your siblings."

Siblings? "Are they here in the Garden?"

"Yes, and you will meet them."

"Well, we have time now to do those things," I kindly remind him.

"I look forward to it."

Gramps returns with my mother, and she and Marten smile as one friend would to another.

"I didn't know," she says and the two hug.

"I know. Everything is settled now," he assures her. "If it is okay with all of you, I would like Coco to come with me to meet her sister and two brothers. And," he says, facing me, "I would like to get to know you and make up for loss time."

Both Gramps and mom look to me for my answer.

"Yes, I would like that," I say.

"How long will she be gone?" my mother asks.

"As long as she'd like."

"I can transport and let you know?" I suggest.

"Okay." She nods, then kisses my cheek.

"It was a pleasure meeting you, John." My father reaches to shake his hand.

"Likewise," says Gramps, pulling him in for a hug.

✦

I didn't know how fun it could be to have a sister. I have been spending most of my time with Hanna although I have had lots of catching up time with my dad. We look like sisters and we are close in age, only a year difference in mortal time. She has a twin, my brother William, and we have a younger brother, Nils, who barely turned seven when the Gathering occurred. The boys look like younger versions of my father, while Hanna gets most of her features from her mother, Melody.

We stroll through the market of Zeta, Hanna and I, carrying bags already full with woodcarvings and trinkets—gifts for my family back in Epsilon. I have never been here in the warm season before. We have always come to visit my aunt during the snowfall. I like it here, especially now that it's become my second home. The style is very different from our tropical lands, and the market is more advanced. Large pine logs are used in the framework of each open shop, and unlike the vendor stands that we have back home, in Zeta there are restaurants that look like small lodges.

A sign carved out of wood and fixed above a canopy reads MOOSEWINDS. The door opens, ringing a small bell, and the alluring aroma of freshly brewed coffee and pastries are inviting me in.

"Do you mind if we go inside?" I ask Hanna.

"Sure, let's do it."

Burlap bags filled with coffee beans line the built-in shelves below the glass case. Arabian music plays softly, setting an unexpected mood. The name and the design of the place seems very American, but the man behind the counter wears traditional Middle Eastern clothing. By Hanna's recommendation I order a specialty coffee named Moosetracks and a warm apple turnover. Hanna gets the same, only blueberry instead of the apple.

"That is my wife's favorite drink," says the man with a dark mustache behind the counter. "Enjoy."

"Thank you," we both reply.

We sit at a window table which looks out into the street patio of climbing clematis and pots of varying sized evergreens.

"Déjà vu," Hanna says, sipping her coffee.

"What is?" I ask, looking around for some sign of what

she could be referring to.

"This is what I was doing at the time of the Gathering. Can you believe it?"

"Drinking Moosetracks at Moosewinds?"

"*No*," she says, rolling her eyes and smiling. "But a similar type of coffee in a similar cafe."

My curiosity is aroused. I had already heard from my mother and her family about their experience, but I would hear everyone's story if I could. "What was it like?"

"Crazy. That's the only word I know to describe it. First, I am sitting there with my friend, Rakel, and we are talking about school like any other day, and then . . ." she trails off. "It still seems unreal. I don't know, Coco. It's like there was a loud noise, and a strong voice said, 'Come.' It shook my body from the core of my being. The next thing I know I am in the air with other people, and we are floating up . . . and then I see him."

Her eyes become wet, and a tear drops from her lower lashes onto her fair cheek. She wipes it away. "He was beautiful."

"Did you know what was happening?"

"Yes, somehow I knew."

"And what about Rakel? Did she go too?"

"No, I don't think so."

"I'm sorry." I pause out of respect before continuing with my questioning. "What did people think was going on?"

"It happened so fast that, like I said, I was just in the sky. There wasn't any time to see what the others on the ground were thinking or doing. I can imagine it though—I do imagine it."

My mom's retelling was similar. They, too, had no time for anything—it just happened. I want to ask more questions, but I don't. I can tell that Hanna needs more time to process everything. I drink my coffee and wait for her to speak.

"What do you think will happen to Rakel?" she inquires.

I give it some thought. "It's hard to say. I'm sure that once you disappeared in front of her eyes, and she began realizing that others did too, her heart turned, don't you think?"

"I'm not sure. We didn't speak much about our beliefs. She may not know what happened. And even if she does know and believes, that only means it will be harder for her now."

"What do you mean?"

"Adamo Nami."

"Uh-who?"

"Adamo Nami. He is the one—the antichrist. I'm sure of it now."

"Give me your hand."

"Why?"

"I have seen him. An angel showed me what he looks like."

"*Okay*," she says, reluctantly giving me her hand. I forget that everything is new to her, even if she has been here for over a month. She may not realize that this is something we can do yet. There's a lot of little things to learn about how our bodies work, even for me in my new body.

"Now bring a picture up of him in your mind."

She closes her eyes and I see the man, the same one I stood in front of with Amraphel.

"Yes, that is him," I confirm.

"Could you really see what I pictured?"

I laugh. "Yeah, let me show you."

I think of a yellow rose from my mother's garden.

"Oh that's cool—yellow rose."

"Yep."

The owner walks up and we let go of each other's hands.

"I'm sorry to interrupt, but I am closing now."

"Sorry, we got caught up in conversation," Hanna tells

him.

"Yes, heavy conversation . . . I hope you don't mind, but I overheard. Your friend that you spoke of . . . I understand. My wife did not come either. I built this place for her. We went on vacation in America, and we stopped at a coffee shop named Moosewinds—she loved that place. Every time we went back we had to stop there to get Moosetracks. I was hoping to surprise her."

"I'm so sorry," I inadequately say.

"I'm sorry," Hanna adds.

"That is kind of you. But she will be okay . . . Yeshua is faithful. I know I will see her again, and I hope you get the chance to see your friend again too."

"Well," I speak up, "Let's pray for them now—Rakel and your wife, and I have an uncle and cousin too."

"That is a great idea," the man says.

We join hands and take turns offering up our loved ones and those left behind whom we do not know. A perfect peace fills the room.

"My name is Arvio," he says. "Thank you."

✦

My mom is standing at the door receiving an envelope from an angel. I wasn't sure if they would be home yet considering it's Day One here. I decided it was time to get back to my life in Epsilon—it's been over a month since I've made pouches or helped by taking teas to market. She shuts the door and jumps when she notices me standing behind her.

"Coco, you're back!" The force of her body meets mine; thrown arms wrap around me and squeeze. She smells like warm vanilla, and I'm not sure if it's her hair or maybe a lotion she is wearing.

"You smell good."

"I do? Thanks."

I thought I'd forgotten the comfort of my mother's embrace, of her scent, but if I had I certainly remember now. Her hand brushes down my hair, and the sound of paper rustles as she lets me go.

"What's in the envelope?" I ask.

"I don't know yet, let's open it and see."

I join my mom on the couch as she slides her finger behind the red seal, breaking it open. She pulls out a white invitation written in shiny golden calligraphy. Knowing the sender, I would guess that the lettering is made of real gold.

"This is it, isn't it?" I ask excitedly. "Hurry, read it out loud."

She sits up straight and clears her throat. Knowing of my eagerness, she enhances the suspense by slowly bringing the paper up to her face and squinting her eyes as if trying to read.

"MOM! You have perfect vision, read it already!"

"Okay, okay," she laughs and pulls me in closer. "Here, let's read it together."

To say that the gold is shiny now would be an understatement. It is more than shiny—it is glowing and pulsating, almost . . . breathing. It is an invitation all right, but it is not written from the heart of a mere human. Instead, it comes from the heart of the one who is the very essence of love itself. Unlike an earthly party or wedding that may take months or years to plan for, this is the long awaited event that has been anticipated for *generations*.

Together we read the words aloud, our voices slightly trembling, knowing the full weight of it's meaning:

"The honour of your presence is requested, that of you and of your family, on the coming Day Five at the time when the blackbirds sing, to attend the Great Feast of which we have all eagerly awaited."

12. REVELATIONS

His face looks the same, only I've never seen him this unshaven. I'm questioning why I even see him at all. I stand as an onlooker, like a ghost in the living room of the small loft apartment. I've never been here, but somehow I know where I am and the full story of what is going on. Uncle Brody sits up on the couch in a familiar green t-shirt and sweatpants, warm from several days being against his body. His eyes are glued to the television as they have been for most of this past week. Newscasters switch in and out to a scene of a man sitting on a throne in a temple, with thousands of people bowed down before him.

"This is just sick," my uncle blurts, throwing down the remote.

"Dad, you have to stop this. Come on, get up," says the intelligent voice of his daughter, my cousin Cheryl. "I'll hear all of the lowdown tomorrow and tell you all about it. *Now, come on.*"

Her light-brown hair is medium length with natural looking blonde highlights, styled and hair-sprayed into place. I haven't seen Cheryl in a long time, but she's the same as I remember—always looking as though she has it all together; the logical one—the deep thinker in the family. Cheryl is a news reporter for Denver's Breaking 5 News, so what she said makes sense to me. What doesn't make sense is how I know other things, like how she and her husband, Reggie, offered her dad a temporary stay once they saw what kind of shape he was in. Or how so many people panicked after that day when their loved ones drastically left them behind a little over a week ago. Now, they spend each day paralyzed by depression. Uncle Brody is for sure—wallowing in regrets, listening to lies of the accuser telling him he is no good. It's not helping that every news channel insists on feeding people with worry and fear.

Cheryl stands there with her hand on her hip, and my uncle changes the channel. A picture of a flying saucer is on the screen with a woman's voice in the background.

"Eye witnesses say the vanishing was caused by Jesus Christ himself, while others hold to their testimony that this was really the work of aliens."

"Can you believe this?" he asks, clearly disgusted. "Aliens?"

"People are just trying to make sense of things, dad. Come on, let's go now."

"Go where?" he asks grumpily.

She shuts off the TV. "To that church, remember? I gave you the flier." She fumbles through the newspapers and collection of dirty dishes on the coffee table until she finds the white sheet of paper, slightly wrinkled and stained with a coffee ring.

"What for? It isn't Sunday."

"It doesn't matter. They are having a meeting to talk about what happened and maybe discuss what's going to happen. I think we should go."

"Those people don't want anything to do with me," he scowls.

"Dad, we *are* those people. They were left too. There's no judgment from them, I promise."

"Argh." He scratches his head and stands up in a stretch, "All right, fine."

"You're gonna change though, right. I mean seriously, dad, you need a shower."

"*Yes*," he says sarcastically, "I'm gonna go shower, but don't think I'm gonna dress up nice or anything."

"Don't worry, I don't think anybody cares about that at this point. I would just like it if you look somewhat sane."

He doesn't find her remark amusing even though he knows that she meant it to be. Instead, he feels ashamed. Hopeless.

By now, I am almost certain that I am dreaming—either that or I am having some sort of out of body experience. I am now outside of a small, white chapel standing next to a sign that reads: Lighthouse Fellowship Church. A black SUV pulls up into a parking space and the three step out onto the pavement—Reggie, Cheryl, and Uncle Brody. They are greeted at the door by a heavier set man in a brown sports coat and jeans. Like a shadow, I follow in behind them.

"Ed Hemmat," the man introduces himself, extending his hand to them. "Thanks for coming."

To his surprise, more people came than he could fit inside the small building. He resorts to opening windows so that those left outside can still be a part of the assembly.

"Well, obviously this place is not going to cut it," Ed starts out, referring to the small building. He awkwardly laughs as those gathered wait for his introduction. "So nice of all of you to come. My name is Ed Hemmat. Some of you I know, but many of you I do not know. I attended this church, which is why I chose the location, but I'm going to work on getting us a larger place to meet for next time. Now, I know this is a confusing time for all of us, and we have many questions and even fears. The purpose of our gathering is for support, encouragement, and study. God knows I need it." He wipes a small tear from his eye. "Uh, I'm alone now, and to be quite honest with you, I can't do this alone."

A couple of voices speak up—"We're with you, brother," and, "We can do this together."

A lady on the third row scoffs. "Ha! You want to talk about alone? I've been alone for twenty years before this and no one has bothered to show me remorse. What did I do to deserve this? You all know that I have served in this church and probably given more money to this church than all of you combined."

"Now, Sandy, this isn't a time for pointing fingers," Ed offers before being interrupted by a lanky young man.

"Maybe you should be thankful you were left here. I mean, what if it really was aliens?"

People begin talking among themselves and arguments start to break out. There is so much commotion now that people are having to yell over one another to be heard.

"STOP IT!" yells my uncle, now standing from his seat. Surprisingly, everyone gets really quiet. "Now listen to yourselves. It's no wonder we were left behind. All of this bitter and selfish talking. This wasn't aliens. It was Jesus. I saw him with my own eyes. He came and did not take us. Now is he to blame or are we?" He reaches down to grab his notebook and turns to Cheryl. "I don't want to be a part of this." He hurries out of the chapel, and Reggie grabs Cheryl's arm.

"Let him go," his deep voice tells her.

Ed follows after him until they are standing outside as I am now too.

"Wait, please."

Brody stops and turns around. "Look, I'm sorry to mess up your meeting. This isn't for me."

"Please, they're just afraid. Give it a few weeks . . . we need you."

Brody sneers, "You don't need me."

"Here take my number. I'd like for you to be in touch." He hands him a small card and Brody hesitantly accepts.

I suddenly jump into a new scene where Cheryl slams the door of the SUV and walks feverishly towards her father who is sitting on the steps outside of the front door of their house.

"Did you walk home?"

"Yeah, I needed some air."

"U-huh." She is mad, but she composes herself and sits down next to him. Reggie's dark frame, now blending into the night, walks passed them and goes inside.

"Thank you," Brody says, taking her by surprise.

"For what?" She is still a little hot-tempered.

"I needed to be there tonight."

"But I thought you said you didn't want to be a part of it?"

"I know what I said and I meant it. But I spent some time walking, looking at the stars, thinking, . . . praying. I've been lying around here moping like a big baby. I felt like such a disappointment, ya know?"

"Oh, Daddy . . . "

"No, I need to tell you this. I did some things wrong. I left your mom when she needed me the most. I cheated on her. I blamed her for . . . ." he pauses, "Jense. I was so mad at

God. I turned my back on him. I decided I was going to do whatever I wanted, so I did. It was selfish. And this past week, after seeing him . . . well, I've just been beating myself up. But tonight I realized some things, and those people helped me to see it. I realized that I'm responsible for my decisions—all of them. All of my decisions in the past and every decision I make from here on out. Instead of feeling like a complete failure like I have been, now I feel like I have a second chance."

"That's a good way to look at it, Daddy."

"Yeah, we all have a second chance, Cheryl."

She rests her head on his shoulder, and together they stare into the vast array of stars. Cheryl tries to remember the last time she stopped to notice them.

"I wonder what they are doing now," she says, a tear streams down her cheek and drops from her chin.

"Oh, they're having a party."

"I should've listened to mom."

"Yeah, me too, baby."

"What's gonna happen to us now? I mean the persecution is getting worse. They are completely taking over." She sits up and escalates into a sort of rant. "How can America be their ally? I don't understand how people became so deceived? I mean, how long before I'm out of a job. You know, just yesterday Danni Evans in New York was fired for refusing to wear a stupid pin with the Order's symbol on it. We were told that everyone in the media are now required to wear these pins to show the world that we are united. How long before they notice that I am not wearing one? Not only will I get fired, but my reputation will be that I am disloyal to government, anarchistic. I will be shunned in my profession as a religious fanatic. But if I do wear it, it means I believe in what they believe in . . . that Adamo Nami is the savior, and that my allegiance is to him and saving the world through him."

"We can't worry, doll." Brody grabs her shoulders and looks her in the eyes. "We just need to be faithful. I've been reading the Holy Book, and as far as I can tell it won't go on much longer. I may not have done things right the first time . . . but this time, no matter the cost, I wanna be ready."

I wanna be ready. I hear it still echoing in my head as I lift up from my bed. "Oh, God, it really was a dream," I say out loud. It's been happening with this new body. The amount of sleep that I get is basically the same as before—about five hours every few days give or take—but the dreams are new . . . vivid, realistic dreams—more realistic than I've ever had before.

Light of morning peaks into my room through the sheer curtains. I rest my face into my hands. *What is this about?*

A voice speaks to my spirit, *Pray.*

Of course, . . . pray. I've determined that what I experienced was more than a dream. It was real, and I was able to be a part of it to know what to pray for, and so I do. I pray for grace, not only for my family, but for all who must remain faithful so that they may endure until the end. I pray for their encouragement, and that they would be reminded that their faith will be richly rewarded. I am just ending my words when a knock comes to the front door.

My bare feet stand on the wooden floor, and I lean into my window to see brighter light shining from around the corner at the house entrance. *Must be an angel.* I haven't seen this many angel visitors in all of my time in the Garden as I have since the proclamation began. I slip on my robe and transport to the front door, feeling revived from my slumber.

"Amraphel!" I hug him and he kindly hugs me back with one arm. In the other he is holding four button down garment bags on hangers.

"For the Great Feast," he explains, extending the garments to me.

"Have you seen them?" I ask.

"It was not proper to look inside. I am only delivering."

"Then come in and we will look at them together."

"Yes, but I may only stay for a short time."

He walks right through the doorway without ducking—becoming transparent as the wooden beams move through his head—and follows me into the great room. I find the garment bag with my name embroidered across the upper right side and excitedly unbutton it to the bottom. Amraphel stands with his hands clasped like a gentleman waiting courteously. It is no surprise to see white linen, but the embellishments are more beautiful than I had even hoped, and I'm realizing that this is not the robe I was expecting. I pull the long gown out from its covering and drape it over a floral armchair. A delicate and soft lace décolletage is beautifully attached to the linen. Tiny diamonds intricately woven inside of the lace catch light from Amraphel's essence. Around the waistline is a feathery sash that ties to the side and wisps down in a combination of soft from the feathers and sparkling from the small diamonds interlaced. Attached to the bottom of the gown are feathery blooms, white like snow. Each bloom holds a large diamond—three carats maybe—as its center.

I am completely in awe and almost speechless. I look up at Amraphel who looks very pleased. "It is unbelievably beautiful," I say. Amraphel nods with much expression in his eyes.

"And rightly so for you," he responds.

"Thank you, Amraphel."

Again he nods. "I must return now."

I was just finishing my goodbye when he disappears from my sight and my mother enters the room, Beverly tagging in after her.

"You literally just missed Amraphel."

"Really?" The dress catches her eye. "Oh, WOW."

It doesn't take us long to pull out the other gowns and try our garments on. They are equally beautiful, yet each are so different with emeralds adorning my mother's high necked bodice and strung pink diamonds hanging from Beverly's waistline. These are definitely not the simple robes that my grandmother and the other ladies spent their time on, yet these were hand crafted by someone, maybe the angels themselves—which would explain what they have been doing since the gates have been closed.

"What about Mark's?" Mom wonders, unbuttoning his bag. She holds the garment up for us all to see and tears begin to well up in my eyes. It is a white fitted shirt and dark pants, but instead of a suit coat, there is a replica of the winged cloak that I made for Yeshua—the robe that I designed and created for him myself, in white linen.

"What's wrong, Coco?" asks my mother. Beverly puts her arm around me with concern.

"Nothing," I say, wiping my eyes. "Nothing's wrong."

I tell them the story behind my tears, from Yeshua meeting me at the Market and having dinner in our home, to my stay at the palace and the breakfast that we shared in the meadow.

"Wow," Beverly says in amazement as if she is listening to a fairy tale story.

My mother looks at me with wonder and now with teary eyes of her own. "I am so proud of you. Not only for the garment—what an honor that is and you did a remarkable job—but for the choices you have made throughout your lifetime."

"I don't feel like I can take any credit, the Lord has been so gracious to me."

"Yes, he has to us all, but you yielded, Coco. That means everything."

It's funny how as a mortal you long for approval, for words of affirmation, and though I receive my mother's praise now I also truly understand that all praise goes back to him, my maker. So I thank him in my heart knowing that he hears me.

✦

A breeze blows through my hair tickling the bare skin of my shoulders. I drop the organza pouch onto the table and pull my hair back into a braid. Chip is dreaming again, hitting against my foot—running in his sleep.

"Oh Chippers, are you dreaming about flying with Gabriel?" Beverly asks, reaching down to pet him. "That's what I dream about."

"You know, you can jump really high . . . that's kind of like flying," I say.

"Not really, plus I don't have any wings."

Jense adds more dried tea leaves to the existing pile between my sister and I. We have a good system going right now. Lion and Letty stamp the pouches and then bring them to Beverly and I to fill with tea.

"Thank you, Jense," says Beverly.

"You are very welcome." He gives her head a shake and her eyes get big, her tongue hanging out of her mouth. She is a character for sure, always making us laugh by her expressions and stories.

"Coco, did you know that my grandmother loves hot tea?"

"I did not know that."

"Well, this one time she was pouring the tea into mom's cup—it was a tea cup with pretty roses on it—and anyway she was pouring the tea, and all of a sudden a dead bee pours out into her cup of hot tea. Can you believe that?"

"Oh man, I'm glad they saw it before she drank any."

"I know. My aunt said, 'Mom, what you trying to do to her, give her lip inchecktions?'"

Jense and I both lose it. It's not only what she said that

was so funny but the attitude behind it and coming from a small child.

"Injections," mom says, walking up from behind us with glasses of water. "How do you remember that anyway? You were an infant."

"I don't know," she says shrugging, unimpressed by her awesome memory.

I keep laughing to myself, maybe longer than I should considering I'm the only one now. I reach for my glass of water and just as I grab it, bells begin to chime.

"Ooh, pretty," Beverly says.

"It's the Opening," Jense tells her.

She gives him a blank look.

Grandma and Aunt Claire appear at our sides, and soon after, Gramps and Mark join us as well.

"We'll go and see together," Grandma suggests.

This will be their first Opening—everyone who came from the Gathering. Our first time was surprising—Jense and I. Gramps wouldn't tell us anything, only that we had to follow him to this really fun swimming hole. We had only been in the Garden for a little over a week and I hadn't imagined that there would be some way that we could still see our family. I'm not sure if the Opening is more for us or for them, but what I do know is that the connections I made on earth were still there—they hadn't changed. I'm wondering how it will be today, for those who are new to the phenomenon.

Sitting side by side along the bank, the waterfall becomes our focus.

"Why are we staring at the waterfall?" Beverly asks.

"Well, Elohim is going to give us a glimpse of earth . . . maybe let us see one of our family members who are still there," our mother explains.

"Like Uncle Brody?" she asks innocently.

"Yes, sweetie, like Uncle Brody."

I'm not sure it counts as prophecy when his face appears before us. He looks much different from the last time I saw him—better. I wonder how much time has past for them. I told Jense about my dream and that evening as our families came together for a meal, he made me retell it to all of them.

"He looks good," Grandma says, patting Aunt Claire's hand.

She takes in air when she sees her daughter then almost immediately exhales her name, "Cheryl."

"Dad!" We hear aloud as Cheryl's lips move. The sound of the waterfall becomes like soft background music, barely detectible.

Jense and I look at each other and then to Gramps and Grandma. We have never been able to actually hear them speak from the Opening before. But now, we hear clearly as if they really are standing before us, like a scene from a movie playing out on the big screen.

13. HIDDEN

Brody and Cheryl embrace as if they hadn't seen each other for some time. I had the dream only yesterday, but the events of the dream actually took place a week after the Gathering—that's been almost three months ago. It's hard to know if what we are watching right now is presently occurring or not. But whether it has happened or will in the future, it is real and it is important since Elohim is letting us see.

"Daddy, I'm so glad you're safe and here now," Cheryl says, taking his bags.

Reggie grabs the bags from her hands. "I'll put them in

your room, Dad. You two have a seat and catch up."

"Thanks, Reggie," says Uncle Brody.

The two walk to the set of plaid love seats separated by a leather recliner; a matching large ottoman sits in the middle of them all. Draped over top is a creamy fur blanket. Colors of orange and yellow dance off of it from the lit fireplace; shadows flicker on the earthen walls. It's a small space with no windows, but comfortable and cozy.

"Well, the place looks nice. Who would've thought you could turn an old mine into underground houses. I guess the others are settled in too?"

"Yep. The hallways connect us to each other. Ed lives next door with the Caffreys, and Sandy lives a few spaces over with the Taft sisters. The supply room is . . ." She takes a remote control and brings up a live feed on the television. ". . . There," she says, bringing up a view from inside a large room lined with stocked shelves. "Everyone voted that Reggie and I be in charge of the supplies, so we and Ed are the only ones with a key. It's full right now and portioned for meals. Every time there is a hunt, the kill will come to us so that we can portion it and store it in the walk-in freezer. Oh, we have a greenhouse too, but Sandy's in charge of that."

"Well, you can count me out of the hunting and the animal cleaning. The greenhouse sounds pretty cool though." Uncle Brody rubs his clean shaved cheek, clearly uncomfortable. "I can't believe it's come to this . . . us hiding underground . . . fired from our jobs because of our beliefs. My grandfather fought for this country to defend our freedom. Now we're just a nation of cowards and bullies."

"Speaking of cowards, how was your visit with Uncle Jim?"

"Hey now, he may be a coward but at least he is willing to help us."

"Really, how?"

"Well, he's agreed to help us pay our taxes on the land, *and* he took the risk of driving me here today."

"*And?*"

"*And* . . . he's covering for us—the land's in his name. He vows to keep this a secret."

"Thank you, God. That's what I was hoping to hear," she says, relaxing into the couch.

"Aw, you know it's only a matter of time before they find us here."

"God will protect us, Dad. I know you don't like the idea of us hiding, but what choice do we have?"

"What good are we down here away from the world? How will people turn if there's no one there to show them truth?"

"Well, what good are we dead or in prison? Because that's what will happen if we go back in the world."

"Let me ask you this, Cheryl . . . if a soldier comes through that door with a gun to your face, will you die for Jesus Christ?"

"Well, yes."

"No hesitation?"

"No, no hesitation."

"So then, if you are willing to die for him, then why not be out there bringing people to truth? And if you die doing it then who cares, you go to be with the Lord, but you save some people too."

"Dad, we have outreaches planned. We will go out a few at a time to the nearby towns. Whoever goes will be risking their lives doing it, but God willing, will return to us safely. It's using wisdom, Dad—strategy."

"What happened to building relationships with people and showing Christ through every day life?"

"We don't have the luxury of that anymore. Now, people just need immediate answers, truths."

"I don't know. Another thing is I just don't like the idea

of being cooped up. I need fresh air, you know? I miss the ocean, riding the waves, sunshine. It's too cold here."

"I understand, but we have to come to grips with the way things are now. I mean, surely you saw the patrolmen on your way here?"

He scoffs. "How could I not? They say they are doing all of this to keep people safe, in order to 'save society'. . . yeah right. That is the lie of Nami and of Satan himself. Their world order is not to bring unity for the sake of peace, it's for control, and—unbelievably—people are falling for this nonsense. I can't believe he hasn't been overthrown yet."

"No, there's no way he'll be overthrown. It's too profitable for all of the governments if they stick together right now. I think some people really are deceived into believing that Nami is the savior—I mean, he is pretty convincing with the miracles and all. But I also think there are so many who are just afraid and don't know what to think, so they are just going with it in order to survive."

"It's just crazy. I would've never imagined this as a kid, not even when you were a kid. How did things change so much in the past twenty years?

"I know, Dad. And you throw the return of Christ in the mix and now everything is really different. But that's what I'm trying to tell you—we have to do things differently. Look, we refused to carry the system. We cannot work, we cannot buy anything. Unless we let that stupid little patch implant on our body, we're not allowed to take part in society. We have a good thing here. We have plenty of supplies stored up to last all of us for at least two years, and with the greenhouse we'll only generate more food. Hopefully, by then, Jesus will either come back or he'll provide for us like he always has." She looks at him with pleading eyes, "Please, just try to like it here."

"Don't worry, Cheryl, . . . I'm staying."

✦

I thought yesterday's Opening was intense, but compared to right now, that was mild. We did a lot of praying together on the banks, and I imagine we will be doing more again today.

Uncle Brody and two others—a man with a walking stick and a red-headed woman—have gone into town looking for ways to possibly talk to people about their faith. I recognized the city sign as they entered, but when I saw what looked like a ghost town I was shocked. I had been there before, skiing with a friend's family. It was a hot spot for tourists with a cute downtown full of quaint shops. As the three carefully walked passed the streets, we could see that the place was completely torn apart from what looked like vandalism. They stepped through broken glass, and glancing into the windows, each building appeared to be gutted out. Every shop was obviously closed for business.

When they approached the neighborhood, the sounds of children crying resonated from the surrounding houses along with the one they began to knock at. A woman opened the door holding an infant and the scene was almost scary— definitely appalling. Pus-filled sores covered the exposed skin of both of their bodies. Before they could say a word she went right to begging.

"Please, do you have any water?"

"Water?" the man with the cane asked.

"There is no water. No one has water . . . please."

Uncle Brody spotted a police car coming from further down the road. "Yes, if you let us in we will help you," he told her.

She looked them over and began to shut the door.

"Wait," Uncle Brody said, stopping it with his hand. "We have water. We have come to help you, but if they see us we won't be able to get you any supplies."

She peeked her head out and saw the approaching police in the distance, then decided to let them in.

"Thank you." They told her.

We are in the same spots that we were in yesterday on the bank. Days could have passed for them or maybe months. We watch them take their seats on her couch. It's a nice house. There are family photos hanging on the wall, one in particular stands out. It's the lady along with, I assume, her husband and two young girls, all dressed in ski gear. The one next to it is a wedding portrait of the beautiful couple, no signs of her current afflictions.

"What is wrong with your water supply?" my uncle asks.

"Don't you know? All of the water sources are contaminated. Some sort of toxin leaked into the Pacific and now it's spread to the other oceans. All of the fish, well, everything in the water is dying. There's dead stuff all over, even in the rivers, lakes . . . everything. It's been all over the news. Whatever the toxin is, they're not able to get it out. The only clean water here is what's left in the stores, but they broke in and took it all. I ran out of everything this morning. I'm out of work . . . I have a baby." She switches the infant to an upright position, being careful where she touches her, then lays her down in a bassinet. "And my other two . . . ." She falls down into an armchair and begins crying and blubbering, "They were taken."

"As in, vanished with the others?"

She nods, hunched over with her eyes closed, tears falling onto her lap. The red-headed woman pulls a few tissues from a nearby box and hands them to her.

"Can you tell me about your sores?" my uncle continues.

She wipes her face then tilts her head to the side giving him a dumbfounded look. "Where have you people been? Who doesn't have sores?" Then as if she's become enlightened, she frantically searches their bodies with her eyes.

"Oh my God, get out of my house." The baby lets out a small squeal but stays asleep.

"Wait, calm down," says the red-headed woman.

"Un-uh, none of you are carrying the system and none of you have sores. You are the ones causing all of this."

"No, that's ridiculous, we are here to help you," Uncle Brody assures her. "Please let me make a call, and I will get you water and even medicine."

She studies him and then relaxes her shoulders. "How do you have water or for that matter, medicine?"

"We have a supply," he says.

She sits there for a moment. "Alright." She walks to the thin, flat touchscreen against her wall and presses a digital button. A small electronic patch on her hand illuminates a series of blue lights into the shape of a star as she connects to a dial pad—the same symbol that Adamo Nami carried. There's a red button at the bottom of the screen—911. They all see it.

"We have water," Uncle Brody again reminds her.

"How do you have phone service if you're not carrying the system?" she asks.

"Someone is helping me. He gave me the number."

"You know, you're putting your friend in danger . . . and me."

"We only want to help."

"And what are you expecting in return?"

"Nothing . . . I assure you. We only came out today to give hope to people. Now that we see your need we want to help you."

I can see belief in her eyes as she begins to trust them.

"I didn't think there were any more good people left. They say in the news that the usurpers, as they call you, refuse the system because they are planning an uprise against the government. They call you terrorists and blame the vandalizing on you because you're unable to buy without the system."

"I promise you we are not terrorists and we had no part

in the vandalizing."

"Oh God, you're fanatics! I should've known."

"Ma'am, I don't care much for labels . . . but yes, we believe in the Holy Book and it's teachings."

"You think Jesus Christ came down and took all the good people? And now what, you're trying to be good now to make up for it?"

"It's not quite like that, but if you'd like we can talk about what we believe, us and you—and your husband even—and we can see what the Holy Book says, and maybe it will answer some questions that you have. But first, I'd really like to make that phone call so that I can get you some help."

"He's gone, . . . my husband. He left me for someone else."

"I'm sorry," says my uncle, genuinely.

"What's the number?" she asks.

The line picks up but no one answers.

"Honey, it's dad."

"Dad?" Cheryl's voice comes through the screen.

"Yeah, sweetie. Look, things are much worse than we realized. We're gonna need water, as in—no one has any water. And medicine, something for infected sores. Is that something you can box up and get to us?"

"Okay, yeah . . . I'll get that to you."

✦

I don't know if I can watch anymore, it's just too hard. But today, as the bells chimed, we knew this may be our last Opening because tomorrow is the big day, the beginning of our celebration—the start of the Great Feast. For old times' sake, Jense and I decided to take our spot behind the waterfall leaving the rest of the family in our regular spot on the bank. Dripping water from our swim, we open our towels out over the rocks, and after sitting next to him, I ring out my long hair.

"I'm ready for this to be over," Jense moans.

I look at him with compassion and rest my hand on his. "It will be soon."

The hardest part about being immortal and seeing into the mortal world is that we know truths that they do not fully know yet. There's no guessing or wondering about our God or what is real when you've been with him and lived in his kingdom. But for them there is still a lot of guessing and wondering, a lot of uncertainties that require faith. If only they could hear us the way that we have been able to hear them. If only they could have an Opening of their own to get a glimpse of our reality.

The rushing sound of the waterfall begins to lower, signaling Jense and I to look into the water as the spectacle begins. I expect to see Uncle Brody or Cheryl, or maybe some of the others who are now living together as a community underground in the thick woods of the mountains. Or maybe the lady with the sores, or others from that town. Are they in any danger—will they be found by the government? I'm sure that Jense is thinking the same thing. We look for their faces or for sight of the mountain community, but instead it is a much broader view. It's as if we are looking down on Earth itself, and slowly it zooms in until we see, like on a globe, Asia and the surrounding areas.

"What is this about?" Jense wonders aloud.

There is a rumbling, and the land begins to shake and move. I have never seen anything like this. I think my heart has fallen into my stomach.

"Do you think it's an earthquake?" I ask, grabbing on to Jense's arm.

"I think so."

The land moves violently, and—like busted seams—pulls apart into three sections, changing the composition from how we had always known it. Everything around it shifts and more quaking begins in other parts of the earth, so forceful that islands begin to move. Disrupted waters accumulate into large heaping waves, spreading out until they reach the other continents and swallow up each of the coasts. My grasp tightens as I watch the world change in front of my very eyes. And just as quickly as it began, so our glimpse fades into tiny particles vanishing into the waterfall before us. We just stare. What else can we do? The earth is literally breaking apart. People just entered paradise for the first time while others entered into their worst nightmare of hell. The end is really coming and my heart aches because although warnings have been sent, people are not ready. But how long can he tarry? How long can he wait before he puts a stop to it all?

The sound of the water beating the rocks below seem to increase in volume and the heaviness of my heart swells. I weep as Jense sits silently. I weep for the souls who have been lost today, and I weep for those who still have a chance. I beg for their salvation because I know that their time really is short. Tomorrow is the Great Feast, and tomorrow I will celebrate and I will rejoice. But today I mourn, and today I plead.

14. THE BIG DAY

Through puffy eyes I see my mother enter my room carrying a bowl and a washcloth.

"I thought you might need this," she says, sinking next to me on my bed. She rests the cool towel on my eyes and I smile.

"Thank you."

Removing the towel, she picks up two cucumber slices, and I can't help but laugh.

"Does that really work?" I challenge.

"These are not earthly cucumbers, these are Garden cucumbers, and you have a resilient body, so of course it'll work."

She convinces me to keep them on my eyes and rest a little longer.

"You'll want to look your very best for this evening. We all do."

My heart leaps at the implication. I picture my dress and think about how I'm going to fix my hair. Should I wear it up or keep it down? And if down, straight or curly? And what about shoes? Why haven't I thought of that sooner?

I'm getting used to wearing shoes again, but I still prefer going barefoot. I only have one pair anyway—a set of running shoes that Mark brought back from Delta, where his parents are living. The shoes do help me run faster, even though I'm speedy enough as it is, but I like feeling the grass and the dirt, the rocks and the water.

Sounds from downstairs echo up into my room, and unfamiliar voices mix in with my mother's. I don't think we are expecting anyone; I would imagine that everyone is at their homes, preparing themselves for tonight. I know that all of the food and wine was delivered to Alpha days ago, and I haven't spoken to Leslie lately, so I'm not sure if she is there right now decorating or if that was already done too.

I transport to face the mirror above my desk and give myself a look. Eyes are not puffy at all, but normal. *Huh, it really does work.*

From the stairs I hear rustling and movement. With my foot, I nudge a small toy ball in my path so that it rolls down, knocking against each stair as it goes. The little bell inside alerts Lansing whom I left sleeping in my bedroom, and he swiftly brushes against my leg to retrieve his favorite toy.

Everyone is moving about. Mark brings fresh flowers into the kitchen, as mom passes by with a vase. A bright light tells me that our visitors are angelic. I join their commotion and I'm welcomed loudly.

"Coco!" says the animated angel with almost florescent orange hair. "We have many preparations for tonight. Are you ready to begin?"

"What type of preparations?"

"You!" he exclaims, overly giddy.

Another angel enters the room carrying long ribbons with real gems evenly spaced down them. His hair is also orange but a darker, deeper hue. "I am Oriel, I will style your hair, and Zakiel here will tend to your mother and your sister. I have made you a bath up the stairs."

"Okay." I am a little disoriented, trying to piece it all together.

"Let's get to it then."

"Okay," I say again, moving back toward the stairs.

The bath smells sweet with cherry blossoms floating and covering the top. I sink into the warmth and relax in the oils. My leg rubs against the other, and I notice how smooth they feel.

A small timer was set and placed on the edge of the tub. After some time, the ding brings me back from my daydreaming, and Oriel's voice calls my name. It's only now that I notice a bathrobe hanging on the back of the door with a note pinned to it and my name written on it.

I meet him in the great room where my mother and sister are sitting under the care of Zakiel, each in their own robe. A portion of the room has been turned into a small salon with salon chairs and small tables holding brushes and containers with creams in them.

"Have a seat here, please." He seats me under a dryer, and within seconds my hair is completely dry.

"That's nice," I say, running my fingers through the warm strands.

"Now this chair." He's so matter of fact, not as outgoing as the other angel.

I sit facing my mom with Beverly to my side. Zakiel

weaves some of the ribbon of diamonds into my mother's hair while putting it in an up-do. Because the ribbon is translucent, it appears as though the diamonds are placed in her hair on their own. Beverly holds the other ribbons and inspects the jewels, then moves them back and forth so that they reflect light.

"Please hand me the sapphire ribbons, Beverly," Oriel requests.

She fumbles through the ribbons to find the right ones and hands them to the angel.

"Are these it?"

"Those are the ones. Thank you."

Oriel is down to business, while Zakiel carries on a friendly conversation with my sister.

"Tell me about your pet rabbit, Beverly."

"Pumpkin?" she asks.

"Yes. The one you made the pretty home for outside."

"My daddy helped me build the fence . . . what do you call that kind of fence, Mom?"

"It's a *picket* fence."

"My daddy helped me build the picket fence."

"Is that so?" asks the angel.

"Yes. You wanna know why I named her Pumpkin?"

"Is it because her hair is the beautiful color of a pumpkin, like mine?"

"Yeah," she says giggling. "You're a funny angel."

"I'm glad you think so."

A brush runs through my hair until it is knot free. Then with a pointed pick, Oriel separates pieces and pins parts of it up. He takes some of the cream out of one of the containers and combs it through, then separates and pins again until the cream is throughout all of my hair. It isn't sticky at all, but smooth, making my hair shine. I feel the tugging and pulling at the top of my head as he intertwines the translucent ribbon of sapphire through my strands, pinning some of it up as he goes, while leaving the rest of my hair down. He loosely curls the remaining hair so that it bounces around me. He takes a different container of glittery cream and this time spreads it on my face until I lightly shimmer.

"Take the rest of this with you, and if you'd like, put it on before you dress."

"Thank you," I say, taking the cream.

He turns my chair so that I face a mirror, offering my inspection.

"It's beautiful, Oriel. Really beautiful. Much better than I would've done. Thank you."

"You are welcome. Here, try these." He grabs a box from a stack of four and opens it to reveal a pair of diamond studded flats. The insides are lined with a cushiony satin. "Your dress is in your room."

✦

I have never been this fancy before, nor have I ever wanted to be. But this is different, and I am enjoying every moment of it. Oriel led us outside to a horse pulled carriage; he stands with hand extended, offering us help aboard. Mark sits tall next to my mother, looking manly and strong, and smelling nice and cologned. Beverly and I sit across from them. She wraps her arm in mine, and the pink diamond bracelet falls to her small wrist. There is still enough daylight to see the other carriages with members of our family and neighbors in stow. We wave overly excited, and Beverly eagerly greets each carriage that we pass. We could've just transported to the gates, but according to Zakiel, Yeshua insisted on the carriages.

The path is lined with lit lanterns, now that the light of day has diminished, and the black birds are singing their songs from the passing trees. As we reach a hill, I can see the lights from the lanterns winding their way up the path all the way to the gates of the Holy Mountain. Fireflies flicker around us and Beverly reaches to catch one. She opens her hand and the bug inside lights up; she giggles. I watch them play around us and notice that the sky is completely full of twinkling stars. Everything feels magical about this night.

The carriage comes to a stop at the gates where Aedhel and Durward dimly glow next to an arch of white and peach cascading flowers. The carriage behind us approaches, and for the first time of the evening I see Jense with his mother and my grandparents. The women are astonishingly gorgeous, and Jense looks very handsome— like a grown man. He allows the ladies to exit first with the help of an angel, then steps down from the carriage with his hair suitably gelled, the white cloak falling down around him.

"My dear cousin," he says with an British accent and takes my hand pretending to kiss it. I swat him away and reach to hug my Aunt Claire. Jense and I both link arms with her, and together we walk through the gates and into the courtyard as the rest of our family follows. It is surprisingly dark in the courtyard, lit only by short hanging lanterns which line the path in between floral plants. I wonder if the softly playing instrumental music is coming from hidden speakers or if the plants themselves are creating it.

From here, we escort Aunt Claire into the City of Angels where the town seems quiet—even with the crowd walking before us up the golden cobblestones. The angels are not here and the shops appear to be closed. The only light is coming from the strung, white lights along the rooftops, the Holy Library included.

The arrival of the carriages were coordinated by the angels so that the flow would go smoothly as people enter and make their way through Alpha. Because of that, the crowd before us are able to walk pretty quickly up the gold, and I am thankful because I really want to get there. At least my shoes are comfortable. Probably the reason I never liked dressing up before was because it was always so uncomfortable.

As we reach the ending of the trees at the top of the hill, a passageway of bright angels welcome us as they play their violins; our eyes quickly adjust to their light and also to the bright light that waits before us. My anticipation is building with each angel that we pass, and *finally*, coming to the last one, we enter the clearing and see the most glorious sight of all.

As far as my eyes can see, covered tables of white linen fill in the spaces of the open fields before the palace. Each table holds elaborate floral arrangements of the same cascading flowers that welcomed us at the gates; I think of Leslie and smile.

Soft peach-colored rose petals completely cover the ground and lead up the center path to the palace where a table and two thrones are placed right in the center. Using my enhanced vision, it is easily visible from where we are standing. An angel greets us and beckons us to follow him. To our surprise, he leads us down the petaled path which ends before the thrones. We look at each other, perplexed.

"Shouldn't we be off to the side somewhere with the rest of our family and community?" I whisper to Aunt Claire and Jense.

"Coco and Marguerite," the angel pronounces, "you are honored guests. Here are your seats." He motions his hand towards a table about twenty feet away from where our God will sit and just to the left of the rose petaled path. I find my name card neatly placed between Beverly and Jense with Mark's next to Beverly. My mom, Aunt Claire, and my grandparents sit across from us, excitement clearly on their faces.

"It pays to know you," Jense says.

Grandma and I lock eyes and smile. "What do ya think of that, *bébé*!" she exclaims, grabbing my hands and giving a good shake.

"Well, hey there!" a man's voice comes from behind and dark hands grab Jense's shoulders and squeeze.

"Hey, Ben," Gramps says, standing to shake his hand.

An angel seats his family to the right of the path across from us. Sena and Eugenie wave to Grandma, Sam and Abby to me and Jense.

"Well, I better go take my seat," he says with a grin. His wife Sarah sees us and waves.

Angels appear and serve us glasses of any drink we'd like, wine being the only thing we must wait for. Out of curiosity I ask for a strawberry slushie, and to my delight, a strawberry slushie I get.

"What are you drinking, Jense?"

"I heard you ask for a slushie, so I asked for a Yoo-hoo."

"Did you get it?"

"It tastes like a Yoo-hoo to me."

"How funny. What else should we ask for?"

"I would like a piña colada," we hear Grandma say. The angel hands her a glass with a pineapple slice over the rim, and from his hand he grabs a pink tropical flower to add to the top of it. "That's really fresh and good," she says, sipping the drink with delight.

Other angels holding violins form small groups and spread out to play their enchanting music around us. People continue to flood in from the sides and from behind us, filling the empty tables. Every community will be here today so you can imagine how curious everyone is to see each other. I search for my dad and my second family but do not see them anywhere.

A man turns around from the table before us with a warm greeting. "So wonderful to see new faces! I am Matthew."

We introduce ourselves and have a brief conversation with him. It doesn't occur to me who he is until after he turns back around and Grandma says, "I can't believe we just met the apostle Matthew."

I examine the tables that are in front of us and on the other side of the path, and realize we are seated right by the first apostles and their families. Spreading out to their sides are the men and women of old. I try to figure out who everyone is. I already know what Peter, James, and John look like, though I've only seen them from afar. But I wish that I knew who Adam and Eve are, or Moses even. I notice two women at the very first table, one in particular catches my eye. She is wearing a crown of flowers.

"Who is that woman, Grandma, with the flowers on her head?"

"That is Mary, the mother of Yeshua."

"Five bucks says that's Paul sitting next to her," Jense bets me.

"First of all, you don't have five bucks. Secondly, that's not Paul, it's John."

"Nah." He searches the tables and then looks back at the man. "Okay, you're right."

With the blow of a trumpet, the doors of the palace open wide, and a hush comes over everyone gathered. I watch the apostles to see their reaction, and it's the same as everyone else—they sit up straight with respect and watch with wonder.

Two cherubim walk through and stand off to the sides of the doorway. My heart flutters as I see Yeshua make his appearance wearing the garment that I made for him. He and Elohim take their seat on the thrones before their table, and the doors behind them close. Off to the sides in the sky, are large projections, like real time video, so that others sitting farther away can see them.

Gabriel comes to stand to the left side of Elohim and

raises his hands, signaling the violins to cease. "Welcome one and all to the Great Feast, the marriage supper of the Lamb!" Drum beats sound and we all shout with great cheer. He lifts his hands again, encouraging our silence. "I present to you our king, and great and mighty is he." Gabriel bows his knee as Yeshua stands, and all of the angels in sight, including the cherubim, also bow in reverence to him. There isn't a person here who isn't smiling or looking upon him with adoration. Gabriel stands, joining the rest of us in silence, and if my vision is correct I think a tear drop just fell from Yeshua's eye. I zoom in closer to see him more clearly.

"I have waited for this day and it is finally here." He pauses and smiles, definitely teary-eyed. "To be with all of you is my privilege. For this . . ." he opens his hands out to us and I see the scars above them, "For you, I have given my all, and now I receive my inheritance."

An angel appears with a crown and holds it up for all of us to see. Inscribed in gold at the base are the words King of Kings, and around the back it reads Lord of Lords. He places it on his head and then bows down like the others. Within moments, the bowing angels disappear and the cherubim resume their standing position behind him at the doors of the palace. Multitudes of new angels come, and carrying a victor's crown of golden leaves in their hands, they begin placing them on each of our heads.

"You look like a princess, Bev," I tell my sister. "And, Jense, you look like Caesar," I say, patting his back. I knew that would get a smile out of him.

Beverly pulls on my arm. "Look behind you," whispers her small voice.

We turn to see multitudes of angels, rushing in from the City of Angels. They carry in large red fabric above their heads, and stretching it out as they lift above us, they create a canopy over everyone gathered. Yeshua reaches for a wine glass and looking at our table I see that we all have a glass of wine in front of us. I'm not sure if an angel came while we were distracted or if the glasses just appeared. As he holds up his glass we follow suit and hold ours up with his.

"I offer a toast . . . to us, the redeemed!" he roars. There is a rumbling, and flashes of lightening flicker through the cloth that is above us. Waves form in my glass from my trembling hands. Together we drink the wine, and strong emotion wells up within me—feelings of gratitude and of completeness.

"Eat, drink, and be merry!" he exhorts, then takes his seat next to his father—the Almighty, Elohim. Just as they came in, the angels along with the canopy make their way out and return back to their city. As the last of the red trails off, our server angels are back with food and more wine. Along with our glasses, there are now white plates with intricate painted patterns of silver along the edge. These are the plates that Leslie and her family designed.

Surely she is nearby. I glance over the tables and finally spot her sitting on the other side of Ben's family, but she isn't looking my way.

The angels bring more food, filling the middle of the tables with meats and breads, vegetable sides and fruits. We are anxious to try them all, so filling our plates we dig in.

"This reminds me of a time long ago," say Gramps.

"Oh yeah, and what time was that?" asks Grandma.

"Well, I'm remembering one Thanksgiving where Claire was holding baby Jense and Nicole was off in the other room with Coco."

"Oh, Coco cried so much . . . poor Nicole basically missed that meal," adds Grandma.

My mom gladly joins in. "She sure liked to cry. I thought I was going to go mad trying to figure out what she needed."

"No wonder she sent you off to boarding school, Co."

Jense is enjoying his chance to pick on me. There are no hard feelings in what they've said, and we all get a good laugh out of it.

"Good one," I say, pinching Jense.

I can't remember the last time I've eaten this much. The angels keep bringing in more and more varieties for us to try and different types of wine as well. I've probably had four glasses. It's nice not having to worry about getting drunk like we would have as a mortal. The most that will happen here is extreme happiness and things may become overly funny. But that could happen even without drinking wine.

We continue to reminisce, and Beverly's stories send us over the top. The laughing is contagious, and Gramps is literally hunched over with his face on the table from laughing so hard. Several times I've caught my crown from falling to the ground.

I would imagine that Yeshua is reminiscing as well, seeing the men gathered around his table now. They, too, are laughing, and by the slap of arms I would say they are telling funny stories on one another. I already recognize a few—Peter, James, John, and now Matthew—and I'm assuming that the others are the rest of his earthly disciples and friends. I haven't had the chance to learn about them yet since my last class with Amraphel took a different turn, but I'd like to know their stories. I try to imagine what it was like for them. There must have been so much pain and heartache that they each endured. But look at them now.

It's amazing how long life feels as a mortal—at times like it would go on forever. I'd always heard people say that life is short, and now I know that this saying is so true for a mortal. But there is hope in that saying. Life *is* short, and the pain *will* end. And then there is new life—new reality that is sweeter than the sweetest day on earth. And all of the pain and heartache that once seemed so consuming becomes only a distant memory and truly a thing of the past. One of Amraphel's readings from the Holy Book replays in my memory:

Therefore, since we are surrounded by so great a cloud of witnesses, let us also lay aside every weight, and sin which clings so closely, and let us run with endurance the race that is set before us, looking to Jesus, the founder and perfecter of our faith, who for the joy that was set before him endured the cross, despising the shame, and is seated at the right hand of the throne of God. Consider him who endured from sinners such hostility against himself, so that you may not grow weary or fainthearted.

I think of my Uncle Brody, my cousin Cheryl and Reggie. I think of the others still left in mortality. I wish that they could see what I see with my very own eyes right now—our king seated on his throne and the joy and the riches that are held for those who will endure. But they will see . . . and soon, because at the very end of our feasting he will scoot back his chair, and together we will break through the heavens with his final return.

15. MAKING MEMORIES

Fragrant air stirs around me as our feet dance upon the blanket of rose petals. We have been dancing for an unknown amount of time—I lost track hours ago. Tables were moved to create open dance floors, where I met up with Leslie and her daughter Evelyn, Abby, and my sister Hanna.

"I'm going to get something to drink, do you want to come with me?" Hanna yells over the music.

I nod and follow her to my table where my father is now sitting with Gramps—where I have spent much time talking to him already. As the song comes to an end, the dinging of glass sounds out from the King's table where Yeshua and his friends are again seated after their own time of dancing. Standing from his chair, Yeshua comes around to the front of his table ready to address us all.

"I want to thank you all for making this as special as I knew it would be. And as much as I would like for us to stay like this longer, it is now time for you to return to your homes and continue your celebrating there. Take whatever you'd like with you and as much as you'd like. Go to your homes and be together with your families for the remainder of the week. There is no need for tending—please just enjoy each other and rest. Our return is coming and everything again will change. In one week we will come back together, and it is then that we will march into mortal land to take back what belongs to this kingdom. But when our feet leave this land it will be the last that we will see of this Garden, so enjoy her now and make worthy memories." He stops and looks at Elohim and continues, "It will also be the last time that we will look upon our Father."

They stare at each other with intense love and a hint of pain in their eyes. Elohim's voice speaks out, all the while staring at his son, "But keep in mind, my children, the best is yet to come . . . and we will see each other again in the New Earth!"

The doors to the palace open and Yeshua turns to face his friends. They join in a group hug, then he steps down to hug his mother. I watch the way they interact, so natural like my mother and I now. He whispers something in her ear, and she steps back laughing then pulls him back into a hug. He kisses her on the cheek before returning to his place next to Elohim.

I take a mental image because soon distance will separate me from my God. The only thing that makes it bearable is knowing that Yeshua will be with us, but a thousand years is a long time. It doesn't settle right with me—a thousand years without seeing him. I suddenly feel unsure . . . and as he begins to walk away, I have the urge to run to him or maybe transport so that I don't draw attention, and I wonder if anyone else is feeling the same as me. Just as I thought I would surely do it, he stops—they both do—and look my way.

Coco, I hear in my mind, *I will be with you. You will hear my voice just as you hear it now. You may not see me with your eyes, but you only need to close them and I will be there.*

I feel him hug me even though I see him standing in the same place before the palace.

Thank you, I say, feeling better now.

I watch them go inside with the cherubim closing the doors behind them, and I just stand there for a moment in his peaceful embrace. Elohim was my father when I didn't have one. He was my friend when I was all alone. But that only reminds me that just as he was there before in my mortal life, he will be there with me again.

I see my earthly father still sitting at the table, and I suddenly feel so rich. I walk up behind him and give him a hug around his neck. He is happy to see me and kisses my cheek.

✦

"Road trip!" Hanna calls after appearing before me and Jense.

"Hanna!" I run and jump into her arms. "What are you doing here?"

"I told you, road trip."

Jense and I look at her with crazy brows.

"Did you get a car?" Jense asks.

"No, but I did get us these," she says, turning to face the woods.

Out from the trees comes Abby and Sam riding on horses, and then Leslie with three more horses behind her.

"We were waiting around for our families after you left the feast, and we got to talking about how great it would be to travel and see the Garden. I mean, we have one week left and I haven't had the chance to see the other communities. I was hoping you all could come along and give me the tour. What do you think?"

"I think it's a great idea!" I exclaim. "Jense and I haven't traveled the other communities much either, and we've been here longer than you. It'll be an experience for all of us."

"Jense?" Hanna inquires of him.

"Well, I wouldn't want to leave Sam alone with all of you girls so I guess I better go."

"Thanks man, you're a good friend," Sam kids.

"So, it looks like we're leaving right now?" I ask.

"Yep," she replies.

"We need to go talk with our families, do you wanna come in?"

"That's okay. We'll stay out here with the horses."

It's been a while since I've ridden a horse by myself. It's not something I ever think to do with my ability to transport and all. Plus, I've never really been fond of riding horses—the only exception being Oleksander with Yeshua, but I wasn't the one in control. As a kid at the boarding school, horseback riding was a weekly class which consisted of me following slowly behind the others. I never could seem to master the balance, and the animals frightened me. As I got older it became an offered elective which I completely avoided, until the last year that I was there. My best friend at the time, Alexandria, convinced me to take the equestrian elective with her, assuring me that I was missing out and clouded by my childhood perception. *And* there was the minor detail that my crush, Jake Phillips, would be in the class. So, I talked myself into it and determined that I was going to like horseback riding. Well, big mistake. I couldn't mount the thing for one, and once I finally did I couldn't control it. Then, after that little incident of falling into the mud at the feet of Jake Phillips, I realized how much I regretted trying.

After my history I never thought I'd say this, but I really enjoy riding this horse. And I'm not sure how I ended up with the most beautiful one ever, with a coat of snow and scattered black dots; I've never seen anything like her before. I look over at Jense on a completely black horse, riding as if he's done it all of his life. They were trained by Abby's family, but she said that if it turns out that we like them, they can belong to each of us. At first I laughed at the idea, but now I'm growing attached to my *Cheval*. It means "horse" in French, but I think it sounds like a pretty name in English.

We decided to start in Delta then circle our way back around. Of course, we only have one week so transporting is still necessary as we go along. After using our code words, "clock it," we materialize on a city street lined with tall buildings on both sides. The boys came up with the term after Jense insisted that we needed something to say when we were ready to transport. It seemed like a good idea and Leslie was quite humored by it, so it stuck.

I'm not familiar with this city—I didn't realize a place like this existed in the Garden. We instantly slow our horses to a walk. People pass on the sidewalks and music plays out from the opening of doors. On the corners are flashy signs introducing upcoming shows, operas and ballets.

"This is Delta?" I ask Abby who's been in the Garden longer than any of us.

"Yes, this is the city, well, obviously."

"Jense, did you know this was here?"

"I've been to the same places you've been, Co—that way, through Zeta," he says, pointing back to the way we came.

"Well, why did we never think to come this way?" I ask

him.

"We had no reason to I guess."

"The whole community is not like this," Abby explains. "This is just a small part of it, but an interesting part no doubt. These are apartments, mostly, and as you can see instead of a market they have storefronts sandwiched in between."

One place called "Gino's" appears to have a lot of visitors coming in and out.

"Hey, what do ya say we go inside?" Leslie asks.

"I'm good with that," I say, and everyone agrees.

It is a packed place with families sitting at tables. Straight ahead a man stands behind a bar-like counter talking loudly to a group of men on stools.

"Hey, hey! We have new visitors," he shouts, and his guests turn to see.

"*Awkward*," Hanna sings to me through the side of her mouth.

Everyone is very friendly, inviting us in, especially the clearly Italian man. "Welcome! My name is Ambrogino, but my friends, well everyone, heh, calls me Gino!"

And I thought Grandma was boisterous, but this man fits the definition perfectly.

"Please, take a seat, and I'll serve you the best food you ever tasted."

We find a newly cleared table in the crowd and try to blend in. I never liked focused attention on me as a mortal, and that hasn't changed much about me here.

Two teenage boys come with plates and bowls, and Gino walks up behind them. "*Ribollita* and *Panzanella*! You will love it!" he says, slapping the table with his hand and walking away.

We are each served a bowl of soup and a separate plate holding a small portion of a colorful salad mixture of soaked bread, tomatoes, and greens. The warm soup hits the spot for me.

"Okay, he's right . . . I do love it!" Abby attests.

Before we can completely finish what's before us, new plates arrive. This time from behind the bar he shouts, "*Bistecca alla Fiorentina*! Just wait until you taste it!"

I can't wait. My tongue immediately thanks me for the tender and flavorful steak, ranking right up there with the meat I had at the feast. Glasses of Chianti wine are befittingly served with it.

"Good choice, Les," Sam says between chewing.

"Nothing like wining and dining," Jense adds in a drawn out voice then takes an obnoxious bite of the meat.

We all look at him, smirking at his unmannered humor.

"What are you excited most about when we return, Les?" Abby asks her.

"Oh, . . . I don't know. I maybe feel a little unsure about going back. Can any of you relate?"

"I can," I speak up.

"How so?" Leslie wants to know.

"I love it here . . . the Garden, our way of life. I guess, like you said, I'm just unsure."

"But there's gotta be something you look forward to, right?" Abby interjects.

"What are you excited about, Abby? I ask her.

"I think mostly just the fact that we'll be free this time— my family, that is. I think about going back to that land that brought us so much pain and knowing that it can't ever happen again to us or to anyone else. That excites me. And I want my feet to get stuck in that swampy mud and lie back to watch the sky without any fear of whips or gators." She cracks a smile.

I can relate to the gator part, but the rest of it I have no clue about. It's hard for me to imagine how anyone could enslave another human being. And to think it happened to Abby who is such an intelligent and beautiful soul is just too unbelievable.

"Do you think it would trigger painful memories to be back at that place?" inquires Hanna. "I mean, here it's easy because we are away from all of that."

"I'm not sure. But pain only reminds me of how great I have it now, and only makes me more thankful."

"Yes, this is true," Hanna agrees.

The same boys return and clear some of our plates, then exchange them with plates of cheese, I think.

"Pecorino cheese with chestnut honey and pears," describes one of the boys.

"Enjoy!" Gino's voice sounds out.

He was right to be confident in his food—he was made to make such goodness. It's no surprise that the place has stayed packed, and really, even though it's a bit embarrassing, it still feels good to be treated so warmly.

Before setting off again, we thank him for the delicious food and for his friendly service.

"Thank you for coming! And happy travels!" he calls back to us.

It's dark out now but lit with all of the excitement of city life. A crowd begins to gather around street performers who are breakdancing and glowing neon colors.

Where to now, Hanna?" Leslie asks.

"Gamma, I suppose," she says, looking at Abby.

"Unless you like sailing? There are good places for sailing in Delta. We could stay here for the night and spend the day on the lakes tomorrow."

"Eh, let's keep going—somewhere exciting!"

"Okay," she laughs, "Gamma it is."

"Should we 'clock it'?" Leslie asks, grinning.

"What do you think, Coco?" asks Hanna.

"I say let's keep riding."

By their expression I would guess that it's not what they were expecting to hear from me, but they all agree to keep riding. So we do, and through most of the night. The wind blows through my hair and I feel free. I look at my friends and understand how blessed I am to have them. They know my story and I know theirs. The story of who we are and what we have experienced. The deep knowing with no false assumptions or judgments. The recognition of value in each one. The way friendship was meant to be.

When the riding becomes mundane we decide to go ahead and transport to Gamma, and that's where we are now. It's still mostly dark, but the sun is starting to rise which means the clouds of Alpha will soon ascend as well. There is some sort of a rumbling sound ahead, and the closer we get it only becomes louder and continues at the same rapid pace.

"What is it?" I ask.

"You'll see," Abby replies.

"Waterfall?" Jense wonders aloud, perking up on the horse.

"It's gotta be," I say.

Dawn begins to take affect and the light of morning slowly rises. In the distance we start to see it. The horses follow the road up the side of the cliff and now it is clearly in my sight. I do believe that this is the biggest, most electrifying waterfall I have ever seen, and the force with which it falls is heart-stoppingly incredible.

"You wanted exciting," Abby says.

"This is perfect!" Hanna responds.

Jense and Sam are already removing their shirts.

"Whoa, hold on, Chippendales," I joke. "We haven't even made it to the top yet."

"Who's Chip and Dale?" Leslie asks. Hanna and Jense are the only ones who laugh with me.

We tie up our horses on nearby trees and walk to the edge. Looking over makes my stomach crazy. "How do you suggest we do this, Abs?" I ask.

"We just jump in!" Jense says.

"*Or*," Abby suggests, "we take kayaks down. Come on, they're over here." She leads us to an open storage, where kayaks of different kinds fill the walls. "Take your pick," she says.

A sunny yellow is my obvious choice, while the others each chose different colors.

"Okay." Leslie stops us before getting in the water. "We should all go together first, and then we each need to take turns staying at the bottom so that we can get a picture of all of us."

"How high would you say we are?" I ask anyone who'll answer.

"The fall is five thousand feet," Abby informs us.

"Excellent!" Jense is clearly excited and jumps with his kayak into the rough rapids.

"Jense, wait for me," Sam calls, getting in.

We hurriedly jump in after to try and keep up with them.

I am rocking back and forth, water splashing in my face. I can see the fall getting closer, and I'm not sure if I should hold on or just expect to be immediately thrown out. I decide to grab the black straps at my sides. Jense drops first, but I can't hear anything over the raging water, and it's getting hard to see as well. I guess that's why I didn't realize I had reached it until my stomach becomes vacant and my heart shoots up into my throat. I cannot yell or move, I can only fall . . . and fall . . . and fall . . . inside of this kayak, heading straight for the open water below. It feels like too long maybe. My face is contorting in the wind, and I wish that I could see to know how close I am, but my eyes are glued shut. Thankfully my hair is in a braid.

SLAM! I finally hit, water shooting up my nose and my ears. It feels funny, good almost. I'm glad that I wore my swimsuit because my clothes would've never lasted. I get out of the kayak and watch it sink. *That was boss, Co!* I hear in my mind and turn to see Jense waiting for me under the water. That's his way of saying he liked what I did, but I can't take any credit for whatever just happened. *Don't worry, I'll get that for you,* I hear his voice again and watch him swim after the fading yellow.

Maybe I'm crazy, but I do it again . . . and a few more times after that—we all do. Not only because Les wants the pictures, but also because it becomes so thrilling. Then, listening to Jense's advice, we eventually put the kayaks away and resort to free falling. That is the most fun.

The rest of our trip isn't quite as exciting as the beginning. I mean, that waterfall is hard to beat. But that's okay, everything is memorable. Just being together, that's what matters. We make it through each community and back to our own—now closer to our goodbye.

We are getting ready to leave the Garden and live on the earth again—mortal earth. I can't help but wonder what it will be like. It has to be so torn apart. And even though Yeshua will rule a peaceful kingdom, there will still be mortal man birthing children who will be born with a sinful nature. How will that work? But the thing that I've been thinking about the most are my friendships. Will I still see them as much as I see them now? And where will we live— will Jense and I go back to California, Abby and Sam back to Mississippi? And the others back to their hometowns? I guess that'll be okay if we are still able to transport, but it will never be the same—not like it is right now. My heart feels a small ache, but I know that it *will* be okay. I close my eyes and go through my photographic memory. At least I have these to take with me.

16. CROSSING

An array of white enters the gates, and we know it is for the last time. Everything stands out when you realize you may never see it again—like Aedhel and Durward, guardians of the mountain of God. I take the mental image and store it away with all of the others.

It's been a sobering morning saying goodbye to Lansing and my miniature horse Dolly, to the plantation and all of the special times that we've had there. I know I will be with my animal friends one day, if not on mortal Earth then in the New Earth that is to come, but I will never step foot on that plantation again. So that is where we spent our morning—

on that front porch—all of our immediate family—drinking Grandma's tea for one last time. I closed my eyes and breathed in the honeysuckle and listened to that screen door open and close. I took in the land, the greenery, not knowing if the place we are going has any beauty left to it at all.

My friends came by for one last ride in the Garden. Abby brought Cheval, along with the other horses, whom we decided to keep together on her land where they could run free and wild. We went to the ocean and sat in the sand, daydreaming about the days to come. And when they had each gone back to their families to prepare for tonight, Jense and I took one last swim in our favorite swimming hole. There is nothing wrong with shedding tears, with feeling pain over the things you love, and this afternoon we experienced those in abundance as we left it all behind.

Now, the time has come, and watching the spectacle before me makes it all the more real. War angels, the ones I saw in this same place months ago, march up the golden road, standing tall above the robed people, each of us making our way towards the palace. I look at Grandma wearing the white robe that she helped create with the gold victor's crown on her head. I notice the set of pink pearls around her neck and I smile.

"Everyone looks stunning, you all did an amazing job," I tell her.

"Oh, my sweet *bébé*," she whines and puts her arm around me.

I can feel her skin against my back where the collar swoops down, and with each step my bare foot peeks out from below the fabric. Jense comes to my side, in the same clothing he wore to the feast—the same as every man and boy. He joins Grandma and I in our last walk through Alpha, reaching his arm passed my waist to hold on to Grandma's hand.

The energy is different today as we fill the open fields

before the palace. Ruby red rose petals replace the peach ones from days ago, completely covering the ground and giving a dramatic effect. The contrast of the white and red is a striking sight and cohesive with the change of mood.

There is no music today, only drum beats starting out slow and consistent, hitting louder as they go, and something builds in my chest, or maybe it's in my stomach. Something I haven't felt since a time too long to remember. It's a cry from deep within, but not the kind I had this morning. It's not sadness and it's not compassion, it's something deeper and more intense.

The red petals brush over my toes and the sweet fragrance mixes in with . . . *smoke.*

In the distance, out to the side of us, the sky becomes foggy with gray vapors, slowly rising into a wall of haze. I search hard for some sort of sign of fire. Instead I see something white, coming forth in the midst of the blur—a man and a horse. Parting through the dense smoke, I recognize the cloak that I made and the white stallion I have ridden on. I see his face, Yeshua, with an expression I haven't witnessed before—passionate, ardent eyes, wild and alive—like fire. He is wearing a golden diadem, with an inscription on it, but it's in a language that I do not know.

"Faithful and True," an amplified voice calls out in introduction.

Every knee bows in reverence, and an awareness comes over me of how worthy he is and how unworthy I am on my own. Everyone must be feeling it because all together we take off our crowns and lay them down before us. It doesn't feel right wearing a crown. We didn't do anything to deserve it. Yes, we kept our faith and we believed, but how could you not once your eyes are opened to see him—once you experience his love and his freedom. He should be the only one wearing a crown. He is the only one worthy.

Oleksander's hooves hit the ground, blowing the red

petals up and around him. It is only after they settle that I realize that the bottom of Yeshua's robe, along with his bare feet, are as red as the petals, stained, as if being dipped into something, stained from . . . *blood*.

"Stand," he says, starting in a low voice and lifting it as he speaks. "And place your crowns back on your heads. You are victors with me, and today we will ride together in our victory."

Loud fluttering sounds out as everyone rises to their feet, like the flapping of many wings. The war angels stomp their feet in unison and lift their hands to salut us. We re-place the crowns but only out of obedience. I feel an extreme sense of honor and respect in this moment.

Yeshua turns the horse around to face the smoky sky, and the vapors begin to form into the shape of Elohim's face.

"Children," his fatherly voice speaks to us, "this will be the last time that you look upon my face until the time of the Millennium has ended. Go with your king and bring justice to the earth, and I will meet with you again when the earth is made new. There, we will never part and never battle again. Remember always, I am with you."

I study his face one last time—the curves of his nose, the sculpted cheekbones protruding below his intense but gentle eyes. A breeze blows through slowly sweeping him away. I try to follow the drifting pieces with my eyes, holding on to the sight of him as long as I can. But he is gone now, disappearing into the thick sky.

Nothing could prepare us enough for today. I know, because we've known about this for a long time. Elohim and the angels have become such a part of my normal life that the idea of living without them for so long is heavy. What will it be like to live in a land without being able to see them or learn from them. I suddenly wish that I would've had more time with my teacher Amraphel. I didn't even get to tell him goodbye.

Out of the smoke, the archangel Michael emerges, compelling our attention. His dark eyes stare out in our direction.

"Watch," he commands, pointing to the sky. It is the first time I've heard him speak. And I've never seen his face looking straight towards me before. I don't want to look away from him, but the sounds of soldiers make it hard to resist.

It's an Opening, a view into the present mortal time. Armies, multitudes of armies, of different nationalities are all joined together wearing the symbol—the mark. The two men that I recognize, one of them I know as Adamo Nami, stands before them and leads them in their marching.

Michael's voice booms over their droning as he addresses us with a speech. The scene continues to play out all the while.

"Who is this that rises up against the one who is faithful and true, and who is this army? Are they not but man, made from the dust of the earth? And, yet, every kingdom has submitted their power and their authority to one man with the intent of killing him who is faithful and true. And isn't that one man controlled by someone else? Someone or some*thing* that has nurtured evil in his heart since before the beginning of mankind. Oh, how clever he thinks he is, deceived by his own deception. Does he really think he is equal to the Almighty God? . . . Today, I will lead my host into the heavenly places, the spiritual realm of darkness, where Satan himself is waiting. And you—the called, chosen, and faithful ones—you will follow our king into mortal land and face this army of rebellion. It is with your very word that you will strike the enemy until they are no more. They will come at you with weapons made from human hands, but you shall only speak one word and it will be to their ruin."

He turns to face the war angels who are standing in full

attention. "What is this word, this weapon from the king?"

In unison they shout, "Truth!"

My insides shake.

Again he asks them, "What is this word, this weapon from the king?"

"Truth!" their voices thunder.

It is completely silent with only the echo from their decree.

Michael engages with us one last time. "From the dust they were formed, and to the dust they shall return. With words all things were given life, and with one word they shall meet their death."

He bows to Yeshua, and in an instant, he is gone.

I now understand the feeling that's been stirring inside of me . . . this churning, this building emotion. It's a war cry, a cry for justice. A cry against evil and against forces of darkness. It is a cry for what is right, and as Michael explained, it is a cry for truth.

The Opening disintegrates leaving Yeshua and Oleksander off to the side still staring—waiting for something. Jense taps me on my arm.

"Do you hear that?"

I listen closely until I do. "Yes."

Repetitive thumping comes from behind the clouds; the sound bounces off the wall of my chest. It's a constant pounding like hooves hitting land and approaching from the grey. The smoke along with a huge gust of wind blows right over us from the force of their entrance. I turn my face to the side and wait for it to subside.

Further than my eyes could possibly see are white horses waiting on a celestial land in the sky. The cries of their neighing mix with blowing and stomping. Yeshua and Oleksander ride out to the front of them, facing us with eyes of fury. His voice rages out above their uproar.

"Vengeance is mine, and my justice is pure! If any are

found with an inclination in their heart for turning, they will be spared. But for those who have set their hearts against me and against the ways of my father, today will be their end."

An angel appears to his side and addresses us, "You will ride, men in front, and women and children will follow. But first we recognize your forefathers."

A large multitude of men step out from the crowd and take horses for themselves directly behind Yeshua. I'm not sure who is who, but I am again wishing that I had one more class with Amraphel.

"Five bucks says that's Abraham," Jense whispers to me, pointing to a man with a long beard.

"Shhh, Jense, " I say, trying to remain serious.

And this is serious, because before our very eyes, a mark appears on the sleeve of their left arm—a red X. I turn to Jense and I see the same mark, stained from blood on his left sleeve. Beverly's eyes grow big.

The angel again speaks. "And now, make way for our king," he says, and disappears.

We begin stepping aside as the crowd parts creating an open space for Yeshua and the multitude to pass. Then, with one last call and final command, Yeshua—holding back Oleksander—shouts, "Men, grab a horse—it's time to ride!"

He loosens his grip and Oleksander is no longer contained. Like a wild beast he takes off to carry out vengeance. They all pass with ferocity—Yeshua and the multitude of horses—leading a flood of white through the crowd, men jumping on back as they go.

We gather around our guys—Gramps, Mark, and Jense— and everything happens so fast. Aunt Claire clinches onto her son. "Find them," she whispers, and he nods with understanding. She kisses him and then pats his cheek. He grabs my hand and I give it a squeeze. Without a word we say our goodbye. I kiss my Gramps and give Mark a hug, then we release them to the milky torrent.

✦

It is dark with only the sound of breathing, mostly coming from the horses. My mom and Beverly ride together next to me, with Grandma and Aunt Claire to my other side riding on their own. There's a wall of light ahead, a portal from our world to theirs. An alluvion of horses have already gone through.

"Will it hurt?" Beverly asks our mom.

"No, baby," she answers. "Remember, nothing can hurt you now."

"I'm glad," she says, leaning her head against mom's back, smiling with innocent trust.

I wonder what's going through her mind and how she is able to process everything that's been happening. I suppose this is only normal to her since it's all that she knows. I try to imagine what it will be like, not only for my sister but for all of the children. Will they go to school with the mortals and make friends with children who will continue to age and eventually grow into adults?

"This is it," Grandma says.

I lift my eyebrows to Beverly, and she pops her head up to watch, then quickly returns it to the security of our mother. *This is it*, I repeat in my head.

The closer it gets the stronger my heart pumps—I can feel it beating in my warm ears. I glance back one last time and see only a small light, and I know there's no going back— only forward now. But strangely, even with all of the uncertainties, the more that I ride the more ready I begin to feel, and somehow I'm even *almost* excited.

Who knows, it might actually be fun living back on the earth, revisiting the places I grew up in. Maybe I'll go to Spain and Venice like I always wanted to do . . . and, of course, Sweden. There are other things that could be fun, like seasons and holidays . . . and cars, not that I'll need them, but it could be fun. I'm starting to see some positives and I'm understanding what Abby was saying. It's like starting over again . . . having the chance to go back and do things differently—a new life.

Yes, I still have a lot of questions, and I'm not sure if that will ever change, but seeing the entrance get closer, and the light get brighter, I know that my answers await. And knowing my God the way that I do, I anticipate a legendary finality.

17. THE CRUX

I expected the brightness; I saw it coming. Like static electricity, the portal pulsated across my body, but even that was anticipated. This, on the other hand, . . . well, . . . it's not what I had imagined.

I clinch tightly to the white reins as the hooves make impact, springing me forward into an upheaval of sand and dust. Granules hit across my face, but it doesn't sting and my sight is not at all affected. I look at Grandma confused and again wish that I would've had a few more classes with my angel teacher, Amraphel. This isn't the coast of California. Why did I think I would return there? It's not even Colorado where my Uncle Brody and cousin Cheryl are living. Nope, this is a desert—a hilly desert. And I think it's night because the sky is dark—vacant really. But because of the light that is emanating from our bodies and the horses, it's as if it were day. I search the sky because I have never seen it look this way. There are no stars, no moon . . . nothing—complete emptiness. I wonder if our coming had anything to do with that or if it was an occurrence that happened before our arrival.

"Where are we?" I ask my Grandma, puzzled.

"Judea."

"Israel?" I ask quizzically.

"Well, yeah, sugar. Were you expecting the Caribbean?"

"Well, I wasn't expecting this."

She smiles and winks at me. "We won't be here too long, this is only where we enter."

It is a rough terrain, foreign from the land I had become accustomed to—the land that I left and will never see again. We follow the myriad of white horses ahead of us and I begin to notice movement and hear shouts coming from all around me. People are surfacing from what looks like hidden entrances in the surrounding cliffs. They call out to each other, and more begin to come out from hiding. Their expressions tell me that they are still afraid and they are trying to figure out who we are. Mothers and fathers pick up their children and embrace them. I look at my mom and Beverly and remember just a short time ago my concerns for their safety, yet here they are with me, forever safe. And now, these people will be safe too because their king, Yeshua, has come to rescue them.

We approach the remains of a small city and slow our horses to a stop behind the others. Rubble covers the ground where buildings and houses once stood. We are waiting, although I am not sure why. To my delight, an angel appears above us, and behind him dimly lit angels fill the sky.

"Close your eyes," he says, calmly.

We obey, and now with my eyes closed, a scene plays out before me, like my own personal movie in my mind. I see the Temple Mount below me, as if I am standing on raised land off to its side. It is filled with many armies, the same armies that we saw from the Opening before leaving Alpha. Although they are dressed according to their own country, they all have a symbol on their hats, a golden star. A line of soldiers stand along the large wall that surrounds the Old City of Jerusalem. They are holding weapons, and I notice that implanted on the tops of each of their hands is the same electronic patch that I saw in my dream; the one on the woman that my Uncle Brody helped. They are facing the Kidron Valley which is below them and filled with men and women, some in combat uniform and others wearing regular clothing—they too carry the system, as the woman from Colorado called it, on their hands.

As I look across the land, it is obvious that great war has come upon Jerusalem, making her desolate. Only the Temple Mount seems to be intact. I then realize that these armies have been warring each other and I am baffled. Hadn't they come to make war with us? For some reason, though, they have all stopped and are waiting for something. Two men begin to lift into the air above the Temple Mount and stop in mid-air. It's like they floated up, but now they stand still—one in blue priestly garments, and the other is wearing a suit with a blue sash draping down his chest—gold toned medal pendants are attached, a golden star is in the center. I zoom in closer and realize that I have seen these men before. It is Adamo Nami—he is the one wearing priestly garments—and next to him his prophet. The prophet speaks out and his voice resounds as if coming from a loudspeaker.

"Listen to your king," his deep voice thunders.

Adamo Nami lifts his arms, the sapphire vestment swoops gracefully down, and very diplomatically he says, "My people." He stands still for a moment letting the magnitude of his presence be admired, then lowers his arms. "You have fought well and we are very close to knowing which country will rule with me in my holy city. But I warn you that there is an evil coming now and we must be ready. We must unite for a time and guard our kingdom." He motions to his prophet and the suited man stretches out his hands toward the sky and it gradually lights up, unbeknown to them, lit with angels. Clouds that were not previously there begin to form, and they become dark and furious, cloaking the light. Flashes come from the clouds and I watch people covering their heads as thunderous bolts of lightening jab down like daggers. The bolts do not reach the ground, rather serve only as a sign of power. Nami speaks out again, "Remember who is with us and who gives us this power, our master Lucifer, the morning star, the innocent one who was unjustly judged by his father. Today we defend his innocence and bring justice to our lord." The armies roar with war cries. Cries of justice for their master Lucifer.

Warm air blows strands of hair against my face. I don't bother moving it, rather I continue to watch this scene, saddened by the depth of their deception. I hear a distant wind, swirling, approaching. The mortals search the sky, their hair and clothing beginning to move as the wind makes contact with them. They all seem surprised by this strong wind, not knowing where it is coming from. Suddenly, with an unseen force, the gathered troops are knocked down, their faces now in the dirt, some making contact with cement and others falling from their rooftop positions, landing to their deaths. Adamo Nami and his prophet remain perfectly still in the sky. The survivors return to their feet in a stupor, fumbling to ready their weapons again, unable to see anything around them until a bright light appears at the top of the mount that is ahead of them. It is the Mount of Olives. The bright white expands, extending across the ridge until the sky is lit brighter than day. I see Yeshua on Oleksander, in the center of the mount, surrounded by his men—our men—and my heart leaps inside of me. I have never been more proud of my family, our kingdom, as I am right now.

An officer in uniform steps forward from the armies in the valley, and a commanding voice comes through a device in his ear. "What are you waiting for?" says the voice, "Go ahead!" The officer gives a signal and rifles begin to fire at our men.

On the mount, Yeshua dismounts his horse with bullets flying past and even through his body, but causing no harm and the holes immediately closing up. As his feet hit the ground the land begins to quake violently. The earth where he stands splits open so that it breaks apart creating a large gap in the mount, and the land begins to separate. I feel the earth below me moving, but my eyes remain closed, watching everything unfold. Slowly, the break spreads down the valley sucking the men and women into its crevice. It creeps toward the uniformed army at the wall of the old city, and this time, by their own choice, they fall down and take cover.

"I'll do it myself," says the voice on the other end, and within seconds the man, Adamo Nami, is standing at the wall of the city along with his prophet, both awaiting the coming quake. The prophet holds out his hand to stop it but it doesn't work. The land is still splitting and heading straight for them.

"I will stop it," says Nami, sneering.

He stretches out his hand and just as it approaches to surely swallow them up, it comes to a sudden stop. Nami looks at his friend and smiles. It appears as if his powers have saved them and in arrogance he yells out, "What's the matter? Have you met your match?"

The land rumbles, and the tombs of the nearby cemeteries begin to quake, but then it stops and everything becomes still, except for the cemetery at the foot of the Mount of Olives. That cemetery quakes again, and bodies, hundreds of bodies, come out from the tombs and from the surrounding earth. They are the resurrected bodies of believers who had been martyred since Yeshua's last return. Angels, carrying special crowns in their hands, descend from the sky above, crown the resurrected bodies, and escort them to a place out of sight, behind Yeshua's army.

"What is this?" Nami mocks. "Haven't you enough men already to take me down?"

For a moment it is silent and the two men scoff to themselves. But something catches their attention from the ground below them. Out from the crack come two angels, both are carrying chains.

Quickly their faces become serious as the man realizes his powers have stopped working. "Shoot them!" he commands his army, but no one helps. The two men reach for guns from the dead bodies near them and begin to fire. The bullets go straight through the angels, to no avail, and they continue their approach.

They try to run but they appear to have become frozen, literally paralyzed. Their eyes fill with terror. The angels wrap the chains around them and lifting their feet from the ground, they take them and transport before Yeshua. They are thrown to his feet, where they bow in defeat. Not by their own choice, but by a power unknown to them. The angels pull them by the chains lifting them so that they stand before the true king. Another angel appears at Yeshua's side, holding a key in one hand and a larger chain in the other.

"Come out," Yeshua says, looking at Adamo Nami.

A dark figure transpires out of the man. Nami's eyes become large as he looks upon the creature now outside of his body. It is Satan himself. The angel immediately chains him and he, too, is paralyzed and cannot move. The two men are lifted up into the sky, and looking into an area of vast darkness I see flickering light afar off. I zoom in my vision as much as I can to see where they are taking them, and the smell of sulphur reaches my nostrils. It is a lake, but instead of water it is fire. The two men are thrown in, screaming in horror. The fire reaches up as if to grab them and pulls them into its depths until the sound and sight of them are no more. The angels disappear and next to the fiery lake a deep, dark pit materializes. The angel pulls on Satan's chain and he has no choice but to follow, but his eyes stay fixed on Yeshua. His expression makes my stomach sick. There is no sign of apology in his eyes, no remorse. Only bitterness and pride. If hate had a bodily form, this was it. Cursing spews from his mouth as he is thrown into the pit and the angel seals it shut. With a mighty voice, the angel declares, "For one-thousand years, this bottomless pit will remain sealed." And then the angel bows toward Yeshua and is suddenly gone.

The same debilitation comes upon all of those left of the evil army so that they too become immobile. Yeshua again mounts Oleksander. With all eyes on him and with a loud cry he shouts the word, "Truth!" The land quakes again, shifting so that the mount below them lowers down to the ground, and I notice that all of the mountains are lowering, even the one I am on. The force of its movement causes the Old City of Jerusalem to lift up making it the highest point in sight.

I suddenly have the urge to open my eyes and I now realize this is real time. I am actually in this spot and looking upon Yeshua and the armies with my own eyes now. Black birds begin filling the sky from all directions, buzzards and crows encircle above. Yeshua lifts his left arm and the horses whinny and move about, ready to charge, including the one I am on.

Again, he yells, "Truth!" and the walls around the city shake and crumble down on top of the army. Bursting forth from the ground at the base of the Old City come rivers filling in the cracks in the earth that were created by the quakes. The rivers sweep through swallowing up the dead bodies in its path.

The angel appears before us again. "This is it," he says. "Follow your king."

Yeshua's lifted hand opens and Oleksander takes off, signaling all of our horses to go too. We spread across the land from three directions and move in towards the city of Jerusalem. For the third and final time he yells the word, and we all join in with him—"Truuuuuuuuuth!" Those left in rebellion immediately begin rotting as the life is sucked right out of them. Their eyes rot in their sockets and their tongues rot in their mouths. They fall to their death and the birds dive down and begin devouring their flesh. The land is covered in black and white.

I have never smelled such vileness in all of my life. This smell I shall surely remember until the very end of time. And as I approach the Temple Mount where the walls once stood tall, rain suddenly begins to pour. My skin soaks it in as a pleasure that has been withheld for some time. The stench slowly begins to fade as the land itself welcomes the skeletal remains into its bosom, the rain washing it down.

I hear a shofar blow and look up upon the Mount to see Yeshua standing next to Oleksander, one arm upon his horse and the other lifted in the air. Men in white surround him. An angel appears and speaks forth, "All ye citizens of the earth, look upon your King and give praise to the one who was and is and who has finally come! He is your God and with him you shall now abide in peace and your souls have now found their rest."

I thought that I would shout out—that I would yell in victory as the others are. Instead, I am weeping, bawling like a blubbering mess. I can't help it, my soul requires it—tears of relief wash over me. I bury my face into the horse's mane. All of the fighting is over and I can hardly handle it. My mind tries to grasp that this is real, that we no longer need protection from an enemy. That we may all truly live in peace in our new world with our holy king. I wipe my face to regain my composure and lift up to see Beverly and Mom staring at me with wide eyes. An unexpected laugh bursts forth from somewhere deep inside of me and in the corner of my eye I see them shake their heads to one another. The rain hits against my face and music sounds out. The beating of large drums resound and an amped up bass joins in. We jump from our horses and start to dance, splashing in the puddles of gathered rain. I now shout and cheer with the others, so caught up in the moment that I almost didn't feel the hand touch my back. I turn to see Grandma and without thinking I fall into her embrace. Again, tears. We cry together and Mom and Beverly join us in our hug. The cool rain becomes warm upon our skin. And as our tears begin to dry, so does the rain. We lift from our huddle to meet the brightness of the sun, returned to her proper place—the sky renewed in her beauty. The brightest rainbow I have ever seen bows out over us. For the first time I feel soft grass between my toes and I hear the sound of birds singing as they fly above in playful swooping. Everything smells so fresh, like spring in all of her glory came forth in one single moment of time.

"Minnie!" We hear someone shout above the commotion and then we see them—our men. With cloaks removed, they walk toward us, their white button up shirts almost translucent from the soaking downpour. Their faces exhibit a sort of champion glow, reveling in victory and the joy that comes with it. It isn't long before I'm hugging my best friend and cousin, Jense.

"Tell them," Gramps says, nudging Jense.

The smile spreads across his face as he locks eyes with his mother, my aunt Claire. He grabs her hands. "I went to them," he says. "I found them."

Tears become visible in her questioning eyes. She looks around as if trying to decide what to do, like a desperate mother yearning for her child's embrace . . . a lover vexed with desire for reconciliation. He rubs his hands over hers and she returns to his gaze.

"I couldn't stay long, but I told them we'd be back soon. Mom, they look good," he assures her.

She relaxes her shoulders and a smile returns to her face. My last memory of my Uncle Brody and my cousin Cheryl was that day watching them in the waterfall. Though we saw them and heard them, still we were left with uncertainty and longing for it all to be over—to be with them again. Now, in this moment, in our gathered reunion, a voice inside our spirits tell us, "Go to them."

✦

The men have been gone every day until evening—Gramps, Jense, Mark, Uncle Brody, and Reggie. I stare out of the apartment window, down at the city below, and I am amazed at the transformation. Everyone has pitched in to rebuild, but not just here—it's what's been happening all over the world. We are a united people, creating a clean and healthy environment for ourselves and our families.

I've never seen so many mansions in one place before. This isn't the Denver, Colorado I've always known. Something happened when we returned—the face of the earth changed, like a rebirth experience. Rivers and streams are now running where they never were before. The violent earthquakes flattened most of the buildings and houses, but you wouldn't know it now. They have all been replaced by newer and bigger estates.

We have one week before leaving Reggie and Cheryl here in Colorado—one week before their log house is finished and the rest of us return to California to build our own homes.

Cheryl walks into the kitchen where mom and Aunt Claire are putting away the clean dishes. She is holding a small white wand in her hand, and an expression of controlled excitement covers her face. She looks ready to burst at any moment.

"What's that?" I ask, walking in her direction.

She turns the wand so that we can see the plus sign on top. Aunt Claire gasps.

"Are you pregnant?"

Cheryl nods with a mixture of laughter and tears. Aunt Claire pulls her into a hug and mom throws her arms around the both of them. They rock with excitement as I stand still, my mind reeling by the whole idea.

A baby. Of course I knew that mortals could still have children, but now it's actually happening. Mortals and immortals sharing a new world together. I try to imagine what it's going to be like. I will stay the same, untouched by time. Cheryl, the baby, they will grow old and even eventually die. It's a sobering fact and I'm not sure how I feel about it.

A noticeable peace wraps around me, like a hug from a father.

"Coco, I'm having a baby," Cheryl shrills.

A huge smile grows across my face and I nod. "Congratulations!" I exclaim, joining in their elation.

✦

"...they will be priests of God and of Christ, and they will reign with him for a thousand years." Revelation 20:6

Dear Reader,

The Feast is the first book in the Feast Series. For more information on the sequel, The Finality, please go to my website to sign up for updates at www.jennyfarr.com. You can also follow my progress on my Facebook page: Jenny Farr.

I hope you enjoy!

DISCLAIMER

The Feast is a fictional story from my imagination, inspired by varying Christian "end time" views and scriptures. It is in no way meant to teach truth about futuristic events. My heart is to share a story of HOPE, a story of IMAGINATION about heaven, a story that shows the king in his rightful place . . . one of ADORATION and EXALTATION. I hope that is what shines from this story and not a debate on eschatology.

FURTHER STUDY

I realize that some of the ideas I have used in this book may be new to you. Below is a brief description along with Scripture references about the topic. Some Scripture references are clear on the subject while others are debatable.

The Accuser: also known as Satan, the devil, the dragon; Revelation 12:10, Job 1:6-12, Job 2:1-7, Zechariah 3:1, John 8:44, Ezekiel 28:13-18, Revelation 12:9

The Antichrist: also known as the man of lawlessness, the son of perdition, the beast, the little horn; 2 Thessalonians 2:3-12, 1 John 2:18, Revelation 13, Daniel 7:24-25, Daniel 8:23-25, Daniel 9:27, Matthew 24:15, Daniel 11

The Mark of The Beast: also known as the number of the beast, 666; Revelation 13:16-18, Revelation 14:9-11, Revelation 15:2, Revelation 16:2, Revelation 19:20, Revelation 20:4

The Gathering: also known as the rapture and refers to being "caught up in the air" with Christ at his Second

Coming; 1Thessalonians 4:15-17, 1 Corinthians 15:51-54, Matthew 24:30, Luke 12:35-40

The Great War: also known as the Battle of Armageddon; Revelation 16:16, Revelation 19:11-19

The Great Feast: also known as The Marriage Supper of The Lamb; Revelation 16:6-9, Isaiah 25:6, John 3:29, Mark 2:19

The Millennium: also known as The Millennial Reign of Christ, thousand years; Revelation 20:1-7, Isaiah 65:17-25, Zechariah 14:3-20, Isaiah 11, Micah 4, Isaiah 2, Matthew 19:28, 1 Corinthians 6:2-3, Revelation 2:26-27, 2 Timothy 2:12

Other references of interest: Matthew 24, Daniel 12, 1 Thessalonians 5, Acts 1:6-11, Philippians 3:20-21, 2 Timothy 3:1-9